It is a strange time to be Black in America; a country where waking up Black is a crime. Walk the journey of being Black in American't, because America CANNOT love Black people, through the shoes of six Black men who reside in Charlotte, North Carolina. Observe how they maneuver corporate America, love, friendship, religion, and even others of the melanated culture. Their journey will make you laugh, make you cry, make you angry, and above all else, make you think. Are Black people citizens of America, which loves to wave its flag and boast of the constitution, bill of rights and emancipation proclamation? Or, are Black people subhuman at the bottom of a caste system, STILL slaves in American't; you are the judge.

American't:

The Corporate Plantation

Written By

King Bell

the Author King Bell
North Carolina

the Author King Bell, P.O. Box 3104, Fayetteville, NC 28302

American't: The Corporate Plantation

For information on booking co-authors for signings, interviews, and other events: www.theauthorkingbell.com or theauthorkingbell@gmail.com

ISBN: 978-1-7374968-0-9

Ebook ISBN: 978-1-7374968-1-6

Printed in the United States of America

To my Father, Lonnie Lee Houston;
the only Black man that I know that reads more books than I.
Thank you for setting the example.

"Shall they use the torch and dynamite? Shall they go North, or fight it out in the South? Shall they segregate themselves even more than they are now, in states, in towns, cities or sections? Shall they leave the country? Are they Americans or foreigners? Shall they stand and sing, "My Country Tis of Thee? Shall they marry and rear children and save and buy homes, or deliberately commit race suicide?

W.E.B. DuBois, 1935

1

WE ALL NEED to unwind after a day of hard work, or no work. But a need to be around people. We need human interaction and touch, away from the cold, mechanical political-correctness on a corporate plantation. The real you needs an environment where no one has a title and people actually have style. Men have swag or no swag. Women have class or no class. I love living downtown because I can exit my building, go left, right or cross the street and there's entertainment, food and art. I can feel the life of the city around me like I'm a droplet of blood in the veins of the street. My city needs me to live, as much as I need it. I'm one with the streets, and I'm one with the city. My city is Charlotte, North Carolina.

Yesterday I went left. The day before, I went right. Today, I crossed the street to a spot called *Poetic Society*, owned by a juggernaut in the creative scene who calls himself Wounded Society. All of his poems share the theme of waking up Black in a white supremacist society called Ameri-Can't. Wounded Society says America cannot love Black people because waking up Black is a crime. The brother is a fountain of wisdom and I like to bend his ear whenever he gives me the opportunity.

I cross the street and stand in line. Wednesdays are open mic nights, and anyone is welcome to the stage for three minutes to express themselves. Booing isn't allowed. When I heard a young, Black brother was looking for investors for a spot for creative expression, I had to inquire and eventually invest. I liked to support the club on a regular basis; although it did well with or without my attendance. Wounded Society insisted I get in free, being a part owner. I explained to him that showing love and support for a Black business as a Black man, required me to pay full price. That's real respect. I didn't want any discounts. And if I ever owned my own business, I'll be damned if I gave away discounts that could put me out of business in the long run. Freebies add up, and are never free for the owners. I got patted down, searched and paid my twenty dollars, and was escorted to a table like everyone else. The one privilege I allowed myself was speaking to the honorary Poet himself, when he had time. Can't lie, sometimes women saw us talking and after he left I'd get some kick back ass. I was going to play that card as long as the club was standing and I was still alive.

I ordered my drink and appetizers just as the lights dimmed. Wounded Society made his way onto the stage to elated applause and cheers. He approached the mic and the show began.

The drum beats lowered as Wounded Society spoke. "You are all adults and have been advised by the lovely waitresses on the rules here at the club. The list is only half full, so you still have time to notify your waitress if you would like to put your name on it." He brought a hand to his forehead, and feigned searching the crowd. "And as usual, I will be delivering the first poem to get the party started. Not that I'm conceited or like to hear my own voice, but I've been known to be conceited and I really do like my voice." The drums banged harder. Wounded nodded and smiled as he witnessed the crowd returning his energy. Wounded considered himself a Sapiosexual mascot. He stood just shy of five-foot-six and was born with cerebral palsy. He walked with a limp and after years of physical therapy, regained the use of his right hand. If you caught him in a relaxed mood, you'd see the right hand turned outward. Wounded wasn't fat but he did have a beer belly, which he said comes with the occupation, the result of being at the club eight hours a day. Because of his popularity, a lot of people were more than willing to buy him drinks. "My name is Wounded Society," he introduced himself. "For those of you who may not know, if tonight is your first time joining us. If you ask why I call myself such? My response is as follows: America can do a lot of things but America CANNOT..." The drums exploded, and then stopped. "America WILL NOT!" Drums exploded again, and quickly stopped. "Love Black people. And even when it tries to love us, it's a perverted love. After loving us or showing the melanated culture love, we, the colored people, always end up wounded." Drums exploded once more and kept going. "Or in jail. Or dead." The drums stopped and the club became silent. "And most of the time, our only crime was just waking up Black!"

Wounded Society's raspy voice was tinged with agony. It sounded like he drank gasoline and chased it with a blow torch that burned the interior of his mouth, his trachea, his esophagus, and his lungs. So, when he spits his poems into the microphone, his words of fervency come through the speaker spouting ashes that cover the audience; a poetic funeral. We may not be able to see the ashes or even the fire on his tongue, but we hear and feel it. He threw back his dreads, eyes closed to the ceiling, signaling the drummer to start again. The methodic beat made me bob my head side-to-side. I knew a mental atom bomb was about to incinerate everyone within its area. As abruptly as they started, the drums stopped again. Wounded began his poetry with gymnastic, vocal chords that could stretched to soprano or bend to baritone, to place emphasis on specific words in his poems. The man spit fire, as he melted microphones and pushed smoke and ashes through speakers.

My society gave me a color
A color that I didn't even ask for
As if I was born with a terminal illness,
I was told I was born Black, now check the realness
Of the situation

So now I'm a walking, poetic demonstration
Of frustration
Of the emasculation
Of my melanated culture
That goddamn white vulture
Always watching me
Hawking me
Stalking me
As if I'm weak, Black and a chicken
Head down, can't fly inarticulately pickin'
Searching for feed, but feed ain't what I need
What I need is recognition that we were once a slave
It's never Black that misbehave
It is your white lies that injure my Black soul
So scared to lose control
Your constitution
Is my pollution
It didn't include me, or us
You said sit in the back and we boycotted your bus
We gave you Medger, Martin and Malcolm,
You gave us BANG assassination
You gave us BANG assassination
You gave us BANG assassination
No more Black leadership
And my soul and society remain WOUNDED!

There were sporadic shouts throughout the crowd.
"Preach!"
"Teach!"
"Say that one again!"

I was born healthy but walk limp and hurt
Your education of my kids ain't worth shit or dirt
That the school was built on

Chapter One

Black kids getting pissed on
Daily for raising their hands with questions
Dodging your mis-direction
About our ancestors they can read, through your bullshit
Keep raising their hands, keep asking questions and oh shit
To the principal's office for being rude
The teacher didn't like his voice, she heard attitude
Since when do kids get in trouble for acting like students?
I guess they are supposed to remain quiet about the struggle like good,
Christian pastors!
Just shut up, sit and stay
Or just shut up, get on your knees and pray
Just don't speak, ask questions or fight back
My society demands that I stay wounded
Because I'm terminally ill with the color Black!

People began standing and applauding but Wounded signaled for quiet. When the crowd has calmed, he placed one fist over his heart and the other in the air:

I will forever jog by your side Ahmaud Aubrey
I will breathe for you Eric Garner
I will breathe for you George Floyd
I will remember your name Sandra Bland
I will remember your name Michael Brown, Jr.
I will remember your name Dontre Hamilton
I will remember your name John Crawford III
I will remember your name Ezell Ford
I will remember your name Dante Parker
I will remember your name Tanisha Parker
I will remember your name Akai Gurley
Let us all remember your name Tamir Rice

After this, almost the entire club stood, and those with lighters raised them high in the air. The crowd looked stern as quiet tears rolled down melanated skin.

I stand wounded but you have all died
And the moment I found out, was the moment I cried
I stand wounded watching them kill you
I stand wounded watching my society burn
I stand wounded watching
I stand wounded watching
I stand wounded waiting for my turn... to die!

And the crowd erupted! The drummer brought back the beat and Wounded Society casually began making club announcements as if he hadn't just completely destroyed the stage. A waitress returned with my drink and I asked her to bring another one with my food. I took note of my surroundings, counting how many women appeared to be alone and how many were in groups. Some new faces some familiar ones. The ambiance is the medication that I needed. Wounded Society exited the stage and was rushed by a group of women for autographs and pictures. I smiled, hoping they'd see me talking to him later that night.

The DJ called the first name on the list and a newbie jumped up from the bar and moved briskly to the stage, with her notebook clutched hard against her chest. She shifted back and forth through pages with frantic anxiety. The crowd grew quiet, and someone called out, "Take your time." Women snapped their fingers. Someone else yelled "We all had a first time girl, we got you."

I closed my eyes, in an attempt to focus on the words of the impending poem – and not the person on stage. Head down I felt hands on my left shoulder. I snapped my head up to see Wounded Society grinning at me.

"Damn bro, I put you to sleep already!"

I stood up to give the brother a dap and embrace. "Never that," I said. "You know better."

6

Wounded took the chair next to me, "Bro we're still here."

"Hey man, this club ain't going nowhere." I stretched my arms out across the audience, "Look at the love you get."

He nodded with confidence. "I'd like to believe our presence at this club, in this city is solidified." Wounded said. "I'm talking about Black people. We still maintain in Ameri-can't. I keep waking up thinking the white folk are going to put us back on the boat and send us back to Africa. And the fucked up part about the dream is that they would charge our black ass to get on the ship."

I laughed and he continued.

"The capitalist mind enslaved us. The capitalist mind imprisoned us. And the capitalist mind charges us for acting like we are free. Ain't shit in this country given to us. Ameri-can't love Black people. They just can't."

I ignored the novice poet on stage. "History will prove that Black people are not even citizens of this country," I said to Wounded. "Or at least that's my interpretation. In order for this to become our country, we need a new constitution that includes us. We need a new bill of rights that includes us. We need a new pledge of allegiance, a new national anthem and a new flag. Until we get that, we just subpar Americans. The progress is not real. Oh! And don't let me debate voter suppression or the *nigger factories*! But the illusion is real. That's why Black Americans don't pay attention to Africa. They think they Black something different. Something unrelated to the shit Africa rockin'. Truth be told, the only minority on the planet is white folk. We eighty percent or more, if we are talking about color on a global scale. I'll never call myself a minority. I know the truth and ignorance is white."

Wounded dapped me in agreement.

When my order arrived-crab cakes and lamb chops with a double Makers Mark on the rocks-Wounded Society told the waitress to bring him the same.

The crowd clapped for the nervous, young lady as she struggled through her first live performance, sharing her poetry with the world.

Wounded pretended to clap saying, "She has potential," he said to me.

The entire time he was talking to me, he still heard and graded every word of the novice onstage.

After my meal, four performances and two drinks later, I couldn't help but smile. Moments like this-good food, with good conversation, and love in the atmosphere-reminded me to appreciate life.

"How's plantation life?" Wounded Society asked me.

"It serves its purpose." I raised my glass with a nod.

"Seeing anybody serious yet, or still running?" he continued.

"I'm not running," I answered. "I've been married before. No rush to do it again. I'm smashing an amazing, married woman at the job. As a matter of fact, I got another married one in my building across the hall. So technically, instead of getting married, I just borrow a married man's wife and keep all my shit when she leaves."

"I learn so much from you." Wounded laughed and raised his drink to me.

"What about you, Mr. Celebrity? How long are you going to play with the poet groupies? Hell, I didn't even know Poets had groupies!" I shook my head.

"Well some of us are more special than others. My mother did tell me that I was special, and she don't lie." He gave me a look as if he just spoke a fact, not to be challenged.

A Black woman that I'd never seen before surprised us both, as she spoke on cue.

"Oh you gon' always be special to me," she said. "I'll kiss, lick and suck all your wounds Mr. Society." Women definitely didn't choose the brother for his looks.

We turned and saw two, beautifully half-naked chocolate sisters behind us. In the club's dim lighting, the women appeared to be twins-and more so because they wore matching outfits. Both were braless in their black halter tops with fat nipples demanding to be seen. And both had belly piercings in their flat stomachs. Their short skirts were high above their knees, with a slit up one side.

The woman closest to Wounded Society bent over to whisper in his ear, while her friend walked around the table toward me.

"Can you escort me to the ladies room?" She asked.

I nodded and stood without speaking. Without words and keeping eye contact, I held out my hand. Her fingers felt soft and silky against my palm. I guided her in front of me so that I could admire her body without her seeing me.

At the door to the ladies room, she turned to face me.

"Are you feeling adventurous?" She asked.

I smiled and said, "I would fuck you on a bag of potatoes in aisle five at the closest grocery store. I don't give a damn about people watching."

She laughed and pulled me into the ladies room by my pants.

We went inside an empty stall with my back against the door.

She sat on the toilet and undid my belt. As the wetness of her mouth covered the shaft of my penis, I got lost in thought. My philosophical mind began a battle with my physical excitement.

I suddenly understood how Black people were distracted from the struggle; between television, the internet, video games, pornography, music, drugs, liquor, sex, white people without guns, and white people with guns. We of the melanated culture are always so distracted that we forget about our own guns. We have never stayed focused long enough on our own weaponry.

Ameri-can't is great at creating distractions.

Less than five minutes ago I was ready to gather arms and sentence my country for murder, theft, bigotry and illegal acts of war. I was arming my mental machinery, reciprocating word play with Wounded Society when I got distracted by the PITS! Yes the PITS!

'*Pussy in a tight skirt*' derailed my revolution before it could begin.

The PITS won again.

I had been anxious to discuss politics with Wounded Society. There was a new history book I wanted to know if he'd read, but the PITS distracted me again!

The PITS knocked me down, got my dick hard and distracted me.

Her hands and mouth moved faster, and my body is tensed for orgasm. I couldn't move or breathe but I could feel my increased heartrate in my chest. My revolution ended in the mouth of a nameless woman. I felt weak; too weak to put my country on trial, to question it, to fight or protest.

The PITS won, and I wondered briefly, if a white man had sent her to distract me from my pending insurrection.

2

....

I'M NINE IN this dream. I get off of the school bus with the pensiveness of a death row inmate walking to the execution chair. I see the door to my house, and walk towards it as slowly as possible. I'm in no rush to see or hear what lies behind that door. As I reached the top step, I can hear my father yelling. I enter the house, remove my shoes and go to my room. Nowhere is safe when the war begins between my parents-except for my room. It is the only place in our home that they have not fought or my mother has had to clean her blood off the wall or floor.

Collateral damage comes in many forms, and at nine, you remember everything your parents yell at each other. Even when you try to forget, some scars live and grow with you forever.

"Fuck you!"

"Leave! Just fucking leave!"

"I hate you!"

All of the angry words they shouted at each other remained with me.

My mother would say "Marriage is work" and "You don't give up on someone you love."

My father would say "Bitches ain't' shit, if you ever meet a woman like your mother, turn around and run. Just fucking run, that bitch is evil."

I'm leaning against my closed bedroom door, listening to the air leave my mother's lungs as my father kicks her in the stomach.

11

He once told me "Don't ever hit a bitch in the face, she'll leave you for that shit. Hit her anywhere else and she'll forgive you."

I want to believe in my young age that I won't grow up to be like him. That I'll never hit any woman.

I hear the front door slam. I open the door to my room, walk into the hall and stand over my mother's body. She's in fetal position taking short, quick breaths. She's crying through closed eyes, and reaches a hand out towards me. And then I wake up.

I always have flashbacks on days that I'm going to see my father. My mother died when I was sixteen. I'd gone to visit my grandmother in St. Louis, and when I got home, my father handed me a piece of paper and told me to read it. It was my mother's obituary. I had mixed feelings as I read it. Part of me was glad that she was free. And the other part of me was mad that she never took me and left my father. We could have gone anywhere.

When I finished the obituary, my father took a gulp from his beer and asked me when the game was coming on television.

"We should be done with that preseason shit," he said, before speaking aimlessly about his job. It was as though I'd taken my mother's place, and had to listen to him now. Or maybe he beat her because she didn't listen. I thought he would take aim at me in her absence but he never did. He actually seemed happy after my mother died; very happy; almost too happy.

After my dream, I stayed in bed for a while. I stared at my ceiling, waiting for the alarm to sound, and thought about my relationships with two married women. One is my white neighbor; the other is a Black executive at my job.

Every morning my neighbor's husband left home at 6:55 and joined his work partner in the car. His wife stood in the window and watched until the car was out of sight, before texting me.

On the days I replied, she'd come over and get her rocks off then make breakfast while I shower and dress. By the time I'm finished, my food is ready, my kitchen is clean and she's gone home.

Chapter Two

The first time we had sex, I was angry at my dead mother. All her warnings to stay away from white women had denied me some amazing sex.

My white girl loved surrendering her body to me. She'd go limp in my hands, like a dead gazelle inside the jaws of a cheetah who'd chased it across the Serengeti. Our sex was rough, but I always tried to be gentle at the same time, to avoid leaving evidence.

My alarm went off at 6:45 am and I waited for her text.

There were women that I distinctly remembered meeting, and there were women that the universe just delivered to me. Since I have no real memory of how our relationship started, I proclaim that my neighbor was delivered to me.

We'd see each other, in passing, but she was always with her husband. The three of us waved, or exchanged casual greetings, but we never had a genuine conversation. Besides, approaching a married woman was against my personal standards; if they approached me, it was game on. I couldn't be accountable for another man's bitch, sniffing her way into my underwear.

I think it started with her husband. I was working out and had my eyes closed. It was my fourth or fifth repetition on the bench. No one was there to spot me, so I went light on the weight, but by that last repetition, I was spent; arms straining to lift that final time.

After getting the weight back on the stand, I dropped my arms to the side, breathing heavy and legs wide open as I laid breathing heavily on the bench, waiting for my stamina to arrive long enough for me to return to my feet. When I opened my eyes and sat up, I saw my neighbor staring at me, literally between my legs.

His eyes were roaming slowly over my body.

I dropped my head back on the bench and said, "I'm almost done if you're waiting on the bench."

I was so tired I had to roll off the bench onto my knees and then, using the bench, push myself up on to my feet.

"I just wanted to make sure you didn't hurt yourself." He gave a light grin and continued to a treadmill.

And then the thought entered my mind and the universe responded. I wondered if he was sexually satisfying his wife? I wouldn't call a man gay for staring at me, something about him made me question his sexuality.

Black men traded scowls or smiles not stares. Maybe he really was making sure that I didn't hurt myself, but if that was true, why didn't he come to the bar and spot me? I laughed to myself and wiped the sweat off of my face and neck. He was a brother, about the same height as me but appeared biracial. By the time I caught my breath and drank some water, he was running with his earbuds set in his ears. I gathered my things and walked back to the elevator, thinking about my neighbor's wife.

I decided he probably wasn't hitting it right, definitely not like I would.

3

....

AFTER MY NEIGHBORLY rendezvous I was ready for a productive day at work. Unfortunately, when I'm productive that means people are being terminated.

I like to consider myself a *Conflict Specialist*. The plantation that bought me, paid excellent money to have me terminate other people. But to make sure to cover their ass, I have to read their employment contract and then find a loophole or ensure specific paragraphs were disclosed to avoid any legal complications after doing so. And no one sees me unless they are getting fired. I'm the last face they lay eyes on before being escorted to their vehicle by security. It's a hairy job, but like my boss says, I got the hair for it. I'm good at what I do because I lack empathy for other human beings, according to the psychologist the company has me see every three months!

Even though we have a coffee machine in the main office, I stop at the coffee truck before I go inside because I like to support small businesses. The white guy who runs the truck always bumps hip-hop in the morning, so I call him Rated R – like a DJ name.

I gave Rated R a nod and ran a hand down my tie. He smiled and started on my coffee, bopping his head to a hip hop track coming out of his Bluetooth speaker.

"Have you heard this one?" Rated R asked me.

I couldn't place the rapper but he sounded familiar. I shook my head, and vibed to the music.

"It's a new rapper. I found this mix on YouTube. I don't know his name and was hoping that you knew."

"I'm not sure I want to know about any of these new rappers. I want to boycott but at the same time, I understand that the baton has to be passed to the younger generation. I'm just not quite sure if I like the direction that they've taken the music. I blew the dust off my tape cassettes about four months ago and was listening to LL Cool J this morning."

Rated R giggled and kept his response to himself.

I paid for my coffee and gave Rated R a salute, before striding to the front steps of the office building. I'm usually early for work, so I take this time to breathe some fresh air, enjoy my coffee and contemplate my daily racial interactions with the white folk.

Not far from where I sat, a billboard asked 'What would Jesus say?' My response was that he repeated the slave master. It was the slave master who gave us Jesus. Therefore, the slave master gave Jesus his words. But the Jesus lovers forget that part. The Black pastor extrapolates biblical scripture like I extrapolate LL Cool J lyrics....'you jingling baby.' Jesus died for our sins but who defines the word sin. Maybe he died for something else or went somewhere else. Like Mars, where the white folk hadn't invaded yet. And after they do invade, will they build a church or Starbucks first?

I glanced at the coffee truck where Rated R continued to serve customers. None of them were Black, so I guess they didn't know who the rapper was either. The mystery continues. But why did he think that I knew? Black men are either all ignorant or all knowing. The opinion of the white person during the interaction decides. Yes, Black people invented all music, but that doesn't mean that every Black person knows all music. I glanced at my watch but instinctively knew it was time to humble myself. I finished my coffee and stood up to enter the corporate plantation.

It is a Black owned company with predominantly Black people. I guess they were obligated to hire some whites for the purpose of legitimacy. The founder of the company, Lonnie Lamour, is also my mentor. I think he's strange because of his off-putting humor, and although I question his intelligence, I have to respect any man who can move his ideas from paper to fruition.

I gave the security guards fist bumps, took the elevator to the eighth floor, and delivered fake smiles and nods to various people along the corridor to my office.

I checked my phone messages first, and then I scanned my emails for important ones. I highlighted six of eighty then notified my assistant that I'd like some orange juice. It was the signal to her that I was ready for the personnel files on the people scheduled for termination.

On top of each folder was a chart detailing reasons for the dismissal. This was critical information because it gave me insight from the people who actually work day-to-day with the individuals in question. One file indicated a pattern of bullying and the other file contained a note with 'GAY GUY' in bold letters with no explanation. I planned to focus on the bully first, but before I started my assistant reminded me of a meeting.

I left my office for the conference room where Mr. Lamour was eager to make his announcement. The company founder had a striking resemblance to the actor Danny Glover, but he didn't share the film star's comedic timing. He opened the meeting with a joke that nearly no one understood. After a few seconds of awkward silence, a few employees gave him sympathetic fake laughter. Behind his back we called him Lonnie *Glover*, as a play on his and the actor's names.

"Today is a very special day," he started, " because we are all alive. But tomorrow is going to be even more special, for those who wake up, because representatives from Wellington Bank will be visiting. Some of you may even get the honor of speaking with them and that's what I want to discuss. I offered to give them a list of executives to interview but they decided to choose at random."

Lamour paused to look each attendee in their eyes.

"I need everyone here to be on their very best behavior. I'm asking these white boys for a lot of *fucking* MONEY!"

"Excuse me Mr. Lamour," I stood up, unable to stop myself from speaking my mind. "We are all professionals here. Meaning we are always on our best behavior. We have the reputation of being the *premier* corporation of Black America. There are no hoodlums or thugs here, so I'm confused by your statement."

"What statement, son?"

"Is it really necessary to tell us to be on our best behavior?"

Lamour stood.

"It's necessary if you planned on doing some Black shit tomorrow. Like loud rap music... or, or... bringing pig feet to lunch.... Or, or frying chicken in the dining lounge. Hell, anything overly Black that would possible offend our cracker friends that I asked to give me a loan for two hundred and fifty million fucking dollars. Yes you are a group of bougie Negroes, but *GODDAMNIT*, even bougie Negroes lapse onto the *NIGGA* side a time or two. And I want to make sure that you don't lapse onto the *NIGGA* side tomorrow. Any day of the week, do whatever it is you do. But TO-MOR-ROW, I need your Black asses to be on your best BE-HAV-IOR !!! CAPESE!!! Any ghetto-tendencies that you may have, SWALLOW THAT SHIT!!!"

I just couldn't help it, having banter with Mr. Lamour was too much fun.

"You're one of the richest Black men in this country. Why in the hell do you need a loan for anything?"

Lamour sat down again and laughed.

"That is about the smartest thing you've said since you've opened your damn mouth, son. This is Corporate America. The land where the quickest way to make a million dollars is to borrow a million dollars. You don't work for that shit. No one works for that shit. Real millionaires borrow the goddamn money. Then we sit back and wait for the next recession. Then when the signs are right, you borrow even more money and then stop making payments. Then the government steps in and says, '*You're too big to fail*' and then they write off all your debt. Through insurance claims, the fed gives the bank you had the loan with even more money than before you got the loan, and then the game starts over again. White folk created this pool, son. I'm just trying to stick a toe in the water."

"I'm not a billionaire because I invented the sun. I'm a billionaire because I have white friends. And when my white friends take out two hundred and fifty million dollar loans, I take out two hundred and fifty million dollar loans. And when my white associates stop paying on those loans, I stop paying on those loans. It's a game. And I want to play the game with Wellington. So if any of you fucks up my ability to get this loan because of some Black shit you feel like doing on a Tuesday, I'm telling each and every one of you, pack your shit on Wednesday and get off my GODDAMN plantation!"

I felt so naive. For so long I'd believed Mr. Lamour enjoyed the ultimate freedoms. But he was just another brother trapped in the game. I wanted to say more, but the meeting was over, and I had people to fire. As I walked back to my office, I played out different scenarios in my mind where I cussed out my boss for his stupidity.

When I got back to my office, Lava was waiting for me. She was sitting on the sofa, and had already closed the blinds.

I could see the steam leaving her shoulders, so I went to my bar and poured a drink for myself.

"What the fuck was that?"

Lava was my muse and my nemesis. She lifted me up and tore me down. She stood five-foot-eight with the genius of Einstein and the gangster-hustle of Jay-Z. She was classier than Michelle Obama and freakier than Lil' Kim. She looked like an Egyptian supermodel. Common men found it difficult to speak in her presence, and her mind intimidated weaker men and women. She had big, brown eyes that could cause a person to hallucinate if you succumbed to her stare. Being fortunate to have seen her naked, I have yet to discover a scar on her body.

And the fact that she cheated on her husband wasn't a surprise.

One man could never satisfy Lava. She wanted more of everything, especially more than the average, mortal woman. She commanded power, with a look, a word, or a slight movement. Lava got whatever she yearned for.

Even though I easily matched wits with her, I wasn't dumb enough to believe I was stronger than her, mentally or physically. No man would be capable.

I didn't believe in God, but if I had, my God would look like her. I would pray to her.

This goddess was my boss. Damn I loved my job!

I took a deep breath and closed my eyes. Then I poured my scotch onto one cube of ice. I lifted the glass to smell the Scotch. I loved that smell. I shifted my stance and looked out the window onto the street below.

"I didn't know Blacks owned plantations."

"Why? What makes us so different from every other race making money off of Black folk? It makes sense to me that Mr. Lamour is still shuffling fo' white folk's money?" Lava did a quick shuffle and turned in a circle. "Blacks owned slaves too. I thought you were the one who was the Black history professor. Or maybe you skipped that chapter?"

I almost thought that I saw a smile as I watched her reflection in the window. "But he doesn't even need their money," I said.

"Oooohhhh Pookie Pooh." She came from behind to grab and shake my cheeks. "No one uses their own money. No one rich anyway. We get rich off of loans we never intend to pay. And then we get rich again when recessions come. The only people who care about economic downturns are people with no real economic knowledge. Rich Americans don't work, they enslave; including rich, Black folk."

She said it so matter-of-factly that I felt a chill run through my body.

Shaking the chill, I responded, "It must be nice to be Black and rich and have the privilege of ignorance."

"Ignorance is white, so too is the privilege of possessing it." She threw her hands up and then placed them on her hips. "Most Black people are too poor to afford the cost of ignorance. You're just disappointed because you work at a Black owned company and thought that made you somehow different. That being here made US different. That your GPS on this planet located you in Wakanda amongst strong, Black warriors, when really, you're south of the Dixie line with the rest of us cotton picking Negroes. It's Corporate-White-America, not corporate-diverse-America. Once you're in, you're White or you play White. It's that simple. So stop limping like you got kicked in the vagina."

"Ignorance of history. I mean GODDAMN! At what point does anyone Black break free of anything white. He has a billion dollars and he's holding meetings with the Black Executives telling us to behave and don't fry chicken tomorrow. What the fuck is that? He's talking to us like...."

"He's talking to us like the scared man that he is. Yes he's wealthy but he wasn't always wealthy. So that means he grew up fearing the power of WHITE just like every other Negro in America. He's corporate. This is a corporation. And corporation means white. It meant white last year. It meant white last month. It meant white last week. And it means white today. And when your sexy Black ass falls asleep tonight and wakes up in the morning, it will still mean white. Think about this, where else can you make this much money doing something that you absolutely hate for the rest of your life. Telling yourself, over and over, I'm through with this shit. I'm not playing this game. But you keep taking the money. Payday comes and you're loud becomes quiet. Then you raise hell for thirteen days and then day fourteen comes and another paycheck. And once again, that direct deposit hits and you're quiet as shit. Whatcha gon' do Black man?"

She over exaggerated her walk, bent her back and gave her best impression of the Black male strut.

"My husband use to be just like you." She smirks. "Coming home every day yelling about what the white folk did."

She became quiet and pensive. She was utterly still, holding herself. Her hands began moving up and down her arms, as if trying to warm herself from an extremely cold thought.

I walked up behind her and placed my hands on her shoulders.

"And then?"

She turned around slowly and began undoing my belt, then my zipper.

"And then he made some white friends who told him to take out a loan. And then one day they came back and told him when to stop making payments."

Her hands were freezing. I shuttered and closed my eyes tight. I then felt the motion of her body falling to her knees. The coldness suddenly became the hot wetness of her mouth.

She made a loud sucking noise with her mouth and then pulled her head away to look up at me.

"And then we got rich. He used to be a history screaming Negro like you. But this is corporate America where Blacks have to assimilate and shut the fuck up."

She took me into her mouth again; another loud sucking noise as she pulled away. "Now please shut the fuck up and think about me, not Mr. Lamour and not about our history. There is something so sexy about your naiveté. You bring back so many memories of my husband when he was younger."

I wanted to disregard that last statement or maybe even respond. But my focus was on the wetness of her mouth. The PITS! There is nothing more dangerous than a focused woman that knows what she wants and is not afraid to open her mouth to get it.

4

....

I WAS IN a delighted mood after my blowjob. I forgot about Mr. Lamour and went back to the folders on my desk. I prepared myself to terminate the bully first. You never know what to expect when you are sitting down in front of a person about to be fired.

You bring back so many memories of my husband when he was younger.

I though of my parents, and wondered why married people seemed to play so many games. I wondered who wins. My thoughts were interrupted when my assistant announced that Mr. Paupau had arrived. I told her to let him in.

I got right to the point.

"Please set the company briefcase on my desk and remove any of your personal items from it. I will also need your badge and any keys in your possession that open any door inside this building. After you have complied, I have some questions for you. Then we will discuss your termination, your vacation time on the books, your severance package and whether or not there will be a positive or negative referral for you from this office."

"What the fuck are you taking about? You're not firing me," the bully declared.

He dropped the briefcase in his hand and charged toward my desk to bend down and toss everything off of it.

I instinctively jumped back out of my chair and to my feet. He took off his jacket and grabbed at his tie, never taking his eyes off of me. I held up a pencil and walked from around my desk and stood in front of him with the pencil between my face and his chest. He had to be at least seven inches taller than me and I'm six foot one.

"You're going to need more than that to stop this ass-whooping." He laughed.

He wasn't fat, just big. He had no muscular definition. I wouldn't be surprised to learn he didn't work out. Men this big usually didn't think they needed to. I'm athletic and fit but he could have easily grabbed me by the throat and lifted me off my feet.

"My pencil has so much more muscle than you" I said to the man, who was six-foot-eight. "My pencil is even taller than you. I'm the man that has to decide how long you get to keep your health insurance. How's your daughter doing with the cancer treatments by the way?"

He looked faint at my question. His chest raised heavy and then fell. He was speechless.

"If you so much as fart in my fucking office you'll kill your daughter. Now I know deep down in all that nose guard frame of yours, you're a father. And the last thing any father wants is to feel like he can't protect his family. So I'm going to say this once and once only. Either you attack me and go to jail without a job, or choose to act professional and walk out of here with some benefits, especially the health insurance you so desperately need."

I was scared, but I maintained my poker-faced demeanor.

"Now, the smart choice is for your big ass to pick up everything off the floor and put it back *EXACTLY* how you found it, and then walk over there and make both of us a drink. Then we are going to sit down like two civilized gentlemen and work out the best course of action for you financially, so that you can still support your family until you find other employment."

Chapter Four

The six-foot-eight inches diminished to something ugly with tears. I couldn't stand to look at his face. I had to turn my back on him, so I walked to the window.

I wasn't sure if he was crying because he was getting fired, or crying because it took everything in him not to throw me out of the window. I felt mechanical. This was strictly procedural. I'm simply doing what needs to be done to keep the grand, corporate plantation machine churning.

He moved slowly at first. His jacket remained the only thing on the floor when he was finished arranging my desk to its original composition. He was about to walk to my bar when I spoke to him.

"The lamp and phone," I said. "Plug them back up please."

He turned around without words and complied. Less than a minute later he was standing at my desk holding two drinks waiting for the man with the powerful pencil to dictate his livelihood once we sat down.

I walked over and extended my hand.

"Let's start over please. I'll act like you just walked in and forget about everything else." He put my drink down and shook my hand.

"You already know my name I'm guessing. I really wasn't going to do anything. I'm really just a loud teddy bear," said Mr. Paupau.

"Being a loud teddy bear is what is getting you fired," I said. "You're a big man. You can't yell and scream and throw temper tantrums when you don't like what someone else says."

"But I'm harmless and I have never really hurt anyone."

"Hurt meaning, you never touched anyone physically? Words cut sharper than swords when thrown correctly."

He dropped his head on my desk sobbing, banging it against the hardwood. I became frantic and grabbed a soft cover book to slide under his head in between the banging.

"STOP IT PLEASE!" I yelled.

"My wife is going to kill me. She's going to fucking kill me. Are you really going to let me keep my health insurance? My daughter has eight more chemo treatments and I can't afford that shit out of pocket. If you're fucking with me I'm going to lose my family. Forget my daughter dying; I'm going to lose everything!"

This situation was getting way too emotional. So I began the termination procedure; "Mr. Paupau, you have 75 days of unused vacation time. Therefore, you will be placed on paid vacation for 75 days, effective immediately. During this time you are not allowed to search for another job. Ten days prior to your vacation time expiring, you will receive a certified letter from the post office with an attorney's card, whom you may call to discuss, should you have any questions. Please take the time to highlight, underline and make notes of anything that you do not understand or may be a cause of concern. Do not sign anything without legal counsel. Should you consult the attorney on the card, all of his/her fees will be covered by the company. If you use anyone else, it will be at your expense. That letter will detail your severance package. You will have five days from the date of receipt to sign and turn in the letter to the attorney's office on the card. You may begin your search for another job after you have signed and delivered the letter to the attorney's office. Should you begin interviewing with anyone prior to signing that letter; your severance package will be deemed forfeited..."

I assumed that his mind was in a fog. Today was not going the way he expected, and he was mentally trying to cope with the unexpected. He asked me some questions pertaining to the paperwork he would have to sign. I gave him the canned response that we were taught in training.

"I'm not allowed to answer certain questions or provide legal advice. However, I do recommend you write your questions down and ask whatever attorney you decide to work with."

Mr. Paupau quietly finished his drink, then walked out of my office.

5

....

NO SOONER HAD I escorted Mr. Paupau out of my office and closed the door to prepare before my next termination, had my colleague, Mr. Caufee, tapped on the door, opened it slightly and stuck his head in.

"Don't mean to interrupt, and I know you like to keep your guillotine sharp, so let me talk fast."

Gravoy Adonis Caufee did not graduate from Florida Agricultural and Mechanical University, FAMU, like my crew and I. He graduated from Fisk University. He is just under six feet, and extremely proud of his home state of Florida. He always wore clothing that somehow had Florida colors or symbolism. He spent too much time trying to sleep with every woman in the building instead of positioning himself as a future leader. He was lucky he didn't work directly for me.

I sat at my desk, frozen in motion, not speaking but looking to inform, with a very distinct expression on my face, that he was interrupting me.

He crept over and sat down.

"Check this out. Have you seen the new, white girl from Idaho? I mean, I haven't met the hoe, but if she like the white one from befo'..."

He threw his head back and grabbed the air with both hands,

27

swaying and smiling as he sang, "My name is Usher baby and I'mma give it to you nice and sssslllllooooowwww."

He started laughing and drumming on my desk.

I didn't laugh but let out a sigh and leaned back in my chair. Gavoy was always comedy, and sometimes he made me laugh when I needed one. But I never felt comfortable enough to take him seriously or let him in on anything personal.

He enjoyed his own joke for ten seconds too long. Then looked at me, extended an arm and said, "I know what you're thinking right now?"

"I highly doubt that."

"Bro, let's double date. You can have shorty that I use to smash on the third floor and I'll holla at the new bag of skittles."

"First of all, I'm not touching anything with such low self-esteem that she actually opened her legs for you. And secondly, do you really want to know what I was thinking?"

"To lay behind a king is a royal blessing. What's on your mind and what's her name? Does she work in this building?"

"I was wondering why we as a people don't celebrate W.E.B. DuBois. Why doesn't W.E.B. DuBois have a national holiday considering everything he's done to move our race forward during a very critical time in Ameri-can't history? I've been reading a lot of Black history and I got an idea that I want to run by you."

"Hold up playa. We at work, so pause that thought and let me get back to my desk before the overseer notices that one of us slaves is taking longer than usual in the bathroom."

He got up and rushed toward the door.

"Ok I get it. If I want to talk about women, excuse me, the hoes, let you tell it, you're all ears. But as soon as I mention Black history, you get concerned about massa.' Aight Black man!"

I shouted to a closed door. I shook my head and laughed. A moment later, I stood up and I opened my office door. Someone I never met before was standing there with a huge grin on his face. He caught me completely off guard.

"I'm the gay guy that you were waiting on."

He walked past me and stood in front of my desk. When I didn't move from the door, he turned around and looked me up and down.

"You look absolutely delicious. Why haven't I seen you around here?"

"Ok STOP RIGHT THERE! We are not doing this. You're going to walk out of my office, and we are going to start this over the right way. You obviously witnessed Mr. Caufee leave my office, so maybe you think that I'm a corporate jokester like him. But I'm NOT! The jokes left with him. Get out of my office and stand at the door until I tell you otherwise."

He looked shocked, but he exited my office as I instructed; pouting the entirety of the walk.

I closed the door behind him. A part of me wanted to laugh and another part of me had a whole lot of questions that may have been inappropriate in a work setting. I struggled wondering if homosexuals were born gay or if being gay was a pair of pants that they took off a hanger and decided to wear.

I muttered to myself, as if trying to give an answer to a thought; some were born and some choose. I walked over to my window and watched a few cars, then a few people. I closed my eyes and took a deep breath. I was finally meeting the gay guy.

I returned to the door, opened it and said, "Good afternoon Mr. Keon Patience. Thank you for being on time, please come on in."

I shook his hand and walked to my chair.

"Please have a seat. I'm going to read something to you and then I have several questions if you don't mind."

He shook his head, again without speaking, doing his best impression of an adult.

"Mr. Patience, you have nineteen days of unused vacation time. Therefore, you will be placed on paid vacation for nineteen days, effective immediately. During this time you are not allowed to search for another job. Ten days prior to your vacation time expiring, you will receive a certified letter from the post office with an attorney's card, whom you may call to discuss, should you have any questions. Please take the time to highlight, underline and make notes of anything that you do not understand or may be a cause of concern. Do not sign anything without legal counsel. Should you consult the attorney on the card, all of his/her fees will be covered by the company. If you use anyone else, it will be at your expense. That letter will detail your severance package. You will have five days from the date of receipt to sign and turn in the letter to the attorney's office on the card. You may begin your search for another job after you have signed and delivered the letter to the attorney's office. Should you begin interviewing with anyone prior to signing that letter, your severance package will be deemed forfeited. Now do you have any questions about anything that I have said thus far?"

"No Sir."

"Do you know why you're here?"

"I'm here because I make people around me feel uncomfortable by my own comfort with my sexuality. I can be extremely flamboyant and it's simply because I'm just happy being who I am."

"You're being fired for an inability to exemplify professionalism in a work setting. You're flamboyancy is viewed as an over exaggeration of your sexual preference. Reading the notes here, you even offend other gay employees. Which is to say that, no one here cares that you're gay, so why the I'M-THE-GAY-GUY-INTRODUCTION? What is going on inside your head that you think that's okay for you to do at work?"

"Being me is being me. Why do I have to be professional at work and me after work? I shouldn't have to be two people."

I cleared my throat and responded.

"Professionalism is professionalism and maturity is having the ability and wherewithal in knowing that being professional doesn't take away from who you are. It shows that you are adult enough to know that there should be a Keon at work, with a very specific behavior, and a Keon after work, which is the take-the-suit-off and walk around in your pajama bottoms and college sweatshirt; or whatever you wear at home."

"I grew up in a house where I couldn't be myself. My dad was always yelling at me to be a man. Walk better. Walk like a man. Talk differently. Hold your head up. Talk like a man. Dress like a man. I could never just be me. I had to fake it for all the real expectations."

I tried to figure out whether this was a sympathy play.

"What does this have to do with the price of tea in China? No one cares. At work you are expected to behave accordingly. Do you really think that you're the only one with a sob story about their childhood? If I got up, opened that door, and asked for sob stories, not only would we get a lot of them, but a lot of them would be a helluva lot worse than yours. But guess what? You can't tell because everyone here is a professional. Whatever you're going through stops at the door when you enter this building and you get your head in the game for the reason that you're getting paid. This is a lesson that you must learn before your next place of employment."

"There won't be a next place of employment for me."

"And why may I ask?"

"Because my husband is going to kill me. Oh pooh!"

"So does that mean you left one abusive relationship, your father, for another abusive relationship, your husband? People do that you know. Hate their parents so much that they go find someone like their parents to love."

"Oh no! My husband is a kind man and treats me very well, he's just." He giggled uncontrollably then raised a hand to me.

"I'm sorry but it is going to sound so corny when I say this."

He held his chest like a church woman.

"I changed my last name to Patience when we got married, and I just laugh whenever I think about it because my husband has no patience. And this is going to be the fifth time that I have been fired in two years. And I just know that he is going to kill me when I tell him."

I didn't know how to read him right then. I saw his mouth moving with this stupid grin on his face, but he didn't seem scared even though he was telling me the worst thing that could happen was going to happen. He almost seemed too happy. We bantered back and forth and I began to feel as if I was repeating myself, something that I absolutely abhorred. I didn't mind repeating myself to a woman but not a man; never a man.

I ended our chatter and asked Mr. Patience, "If he had any business-related questions for me?" Everything he asked was of a personal nature and I declined answering. Finally, he sat for a few minutes in silence and then stood to gather himself. He left without the gayety that he once tried to enter.

I walked over to my bar to make a drink, then moved to the window overlooking downtown and replayed the strange interaction with the Gay Guy.

I remembered my first crush. Her name was Tiffany and we were in third grade and she was taller than me. She was the first girl that I'd wanted to kiss on purpose. I thought she was the prettiest girl in school. I laughed to myself, thinking about how fast time flies. Then I wondered, if Keon thought about boys in the third grade, or did he become gay later?

6

....

ALL OF MY FAMU brothers worked in downtown Charlotte, so it was not unusual for my assistant to inform me that I had an impromptu visitor, and ask if she could give security permission to allow them entry. It was only ever one visitor, and today it was KayBee.

Mr. Kavonnie Brix was standing on the grounds of the corporate plantation. It took about twelve minutes to get to my office from security, so I had time to put away my paperwork.

My assistant lightly tapped on my door, and allowed KayBee into my office. After she shut the door, I stood and extended a fist bump to my friend.

"Black man how you doin'?"

He opened the folder he was holding and handed me a piece of folded paper.

"In case you want to review it," he said. Before I even finished unfolding it, KayBee had started laughing. "It's my liberty pass from my massa' over at Lee & Perry."

I crumpled the single piece of paper and threw it at him as he sat down.

Kavonnie is five-feet eleven, and when he turns around, no matter what he is wearing, he has the perfect upside-down triangle; wide, muscular shoulders, and a zero-fat torso ended in a tight

33

waist that extended out to perfectly fit legs. The brother was a gym beast and although he dreamed of playing football at Florida State University, he didn't have the grades for it.

"Seriously, what's going on?"

I took my seat. Smiling and shaking my head, I clasped my hands on my desk. He stroked his beard and tilted his head to the right. I remained silent with anticipation of the performance. The utter story-telling capability of the Black man is unlike any other race, pertaining to emotion and animation. I couldn't help but laugh.

"Come on man, I know you didn't come here just to stare at me and stroke your damn beard; spit it out!"

"Check this out right." He moved his chair close enough to my desk so that he could fold his arms on top of it. Then he asked me "Have you ever ate some pussy and had the girl nut in your beard and then you go kiss another girl and she smells it, but before she can ask about the pussy juice, you tell her its beard lotion?"

He delivered the question with a stoic, straight face and looked me in the eyes, without blinking, as he waited for my reply.

"Hold on please. Let's put the question in reverse and examine what the hell you just said to me. I'm not perfect by any means, but there are just life rules I expect everyone to know and follow. You're supposed to wash your ass and mouth after doing some freaky shit. You let a woman, not your wife obviously, but some other woman vagina smash your face, nut in your beard and then you went to see another woman, or are you talking about your wife being the other woman?"

"Err my wife, Bro. These side bitches expensive. I can only afford one at a time. And anyway, I like when my side-boo nuts in my beard. This is beard life and what greater lotion can a man ask for than a woman's pussy juice? It's the greatest aphrodisiac. Now check this out, this is the best part."

He looked to his left and then his right, as if necessary.

"And she's a squirter, Bro!"

He pumped his arms in the air.

I stood up again.

"So now we just went from she nutted in your beard to she pissed in your face. That's not pussy juice. That's PISS!"

"She's a squirter. I make her nut just by touching her. Bro, look at my beard."

He turned to the side and tilted his head back, chin jutted, to accentuate his perfectly groomed beard.

"No negro. Hell naw. I've been with squirters and that is piss. Cum is cum and piss is piss. If it smells like piss it is piss. You let a woman vagina smash you in the face and piss in your beard and then you went home to your wife. YOU ARE ASKING TO BE KILLED! How are you even still alive? Is this why you married WHITE? KayBee listen please. We all know you got the lowest grades at FAMU but you graduated. That means there is a brain somewhere in there."

"You're hating on beard life right now and it's absolutely disgusting. I knew you were the wrong person to ask this question."

"Are you not a Jesus lover?" I asked.

"Of course!"

"Personally, I don't read the book of weaponry. However, is it not one of the commandments that specifically state '*THOU SHALL WASHETH THY ASSETH*'especially after sex."

"Err... I read the bible but I don't go around memorizing scripture so that I can shoot people with the word and my judgment."

"Somewhere in the book of weaponry has to be a statement on cleanliness. After all, didn't Jesus invent toilet paper?"

This entire conversation caught me off guard.

"Why would my God invent toilet paper?"

"Because your God is full of SSSSHHHHIIIIITTTTTTTT!" I fell back in my chair and laughed so hard I almost fell backwards onto the floor. "How did you just fall for that one?" That's the first atheist joke I ever learned. Anyway, I'm sure your Jesus would be happier watching you get some ass and then getting in the shower is my point."

He threw his hands at me.

"Bro, have you not done some FREAKY EAKY? Don't you have some kinky, adventurous shit you like, that you hope nobody ever finds? Something that you can only share with your BOYS! Your brothers!" He went back to stroking his beard. "I'm sharing right now, the wonders of beard life."

"Listen to me please. I don't care when I have sex or where I have sex but I do know that I will shower after it, or as soon as I possibly can. I am a GERM-A-PHOBE! It is a must for me. Cleanliness is blackness Black man! And what about your wife?"

He ignored my last question.

"And you eat pussy right?"

"Yes, I eat the pink meat when it don't stink. But again, afterwards, I gargle with peroxide, brush my teeth and then gargle with mouthwash to ensure cleanliness. I would take off running if the interaction with another woman would lead to her wanting a kiss, knowing what I just did with another woman. To hell with beard life, I want CLEAN life. I'm looking at your beard right now and I think it has a yeast infection."

I leaned on the desk to peer closer at KayBee. He was already ignoring me. He was back to stroking his beard and replaying getting peed on. His mind was elsewhere, a smile across his face.

"Please tell me that asking me that question is not the only reason you came here?"

"No sir. Lee & Perry are riding the coat tail of Wellington & Wellington. Working at a Black owned bank, we have to get in where we fit in. They don't want to lend Mr. Lamour the full amount that he's trying to obtain. So we have committed to providing a second lien position at an undisclosed amount."

"Undisclosed amount meaning?" I asked, still trying to figure out why billionaires take out loans.

"Meaning, whatever the white boys don't give him, we pick up the slack. Second lien position means a lot of fees and a double-digit interest rate. It works in our favor twice. First of all, we make a lot of money off of a transaction like this. Secondly, having him in our portfolio brings other high dollar clients to our bank."

"But why would he do that?" I was curious.

"Why does anyone make the decisions they make with their money? He's a smart man, so I'm sure that he has a plan; even if we can't see it. All he makes are boss moves. Besides, he can afford it. And if a bank allowed you to play with their money and hold onto yours, wouldn't you do that?"

"True dat. True dat." I agreed. "It's hard to get mad at a Black billionaire in Ameri-can't. I don't always like how he speaks to us but I'll salute him forever."

KayBee jumped up suddenly.

"Bro, you good?"

"I just thought about Sadikki. He still works here, right?"

"Oh yeah. I don't talk to him as much, since I got promoted to the eighth floor. But he's still down there with the field Negroes. The brother had a chance to get promoted and turned it down. Claiming he didn't want the responsibility. And that makes absolutely no sense to me. What is the sense of working if you're not working toward a higher goal?"

"Being selfish, you're only thinking about you. Maybe he found happiness at the level he's at, or maybe the level he's at was his 'highest' goal."

"Would you choose happiness over money?" I asked.

"Actually I would, and Sadikki has a beard. I should have gone to him in the first place. Men with beards are smarter than men without them."

"You are sick. And for future reference, when we embrace, DO-NOT-LET-THAT-BEARD-TOUCH-MY-FACE! Because if it does, I'm going to seriously injure at least eight of your ribs. And tell skittles I said hello."

I smiled and imitated that I was stroking a beard like his.

"FUCK YOU! You baby faced bastard. BEARD LIFE FOREVER! It's a sad world when a brother like yourself is hating on beards and squirters."

KayBee shook his head and walked confidently towards the door.

I stood up again.

"Only because we're boys I'm going to say this. And I mean it from the bottom of my nut sack. Bro, if you want me to pee on you, I'll at least think about it."

We both cracked up with laughter. He was trying to come back at me with a comical rebuttal but couldn't get it out.

Finally, he said, "You got me Bro. You got me. I'll see you later in the week. Bowden Ballers!"

"Bowden Ballers," I replied, wiping tears of laughter from my eyes as I watched my college brother exit my office.

7

·················

KAYBEE TOOK THE elevator to the 2nd floor, still smiling to himself at the jokes he'd just shared with his friend upstairs. When he got off the elevator, he looked around curiously, unsure of where his other friend's office was.

A woman stood up and asked, "May I help you?"

"Yes, uh, good afternoon. I'm Mr. Brix here to see Mr. Sadikki please."

The woman smiled and escorted him to a cubicle where a man sat bobbing his head with headphones on; oblivious to the world. The woman left and Kavonnie nudged his associate on the shoulder.

After ten minutes of beard stroking and jokes, Kaybee asked, "What's up with Knowledge telling me that you declined a promotion? Not getting in your business but I don't want to assume either. I've seen people decline for various reasons and just curious Bro."

Sadikki leaned in close and lowered his voice.

"I got diagnosed with some serious shit that only affects Black people. The promotion would have required me to give all of these presentations and travel to different conferences. YO! I can't be in a room full of white folk. I get to hyperventilating. The hair stands up all over my body. I start hearing whips cracking and people screaming. I have visions of running from dogs and horses chasing me. I even have visions of the white folk preparing to lynch me."

39

"But why?"

"The psychologist said I suffer from P-T-S-S Bro, 'Post Traumatic Slave Syndrome.' Actually, all Blacks do if they were born in this country. It just affects all of us differently."

Sadikki leaned back in his chair and nodded.

"Yep! Shit is real outside. You need to peep game and read Post Traumatic Slave Syndrome by Dr. Joy DeGruy. And the medical industry on the hush because they don't give a fuck about us number one. And number two, if this shit went public, it would be more dynamite in the reparations fire pit. All white psychologists will laugh and act like they never heard of it, or tell you it's Black lore. But you sit down with any brother or sister in the profession and they know what's up."

"And with all the protests taking place, sometimes I have anxiety attacks just sitting by myself. Is it a conspiracy against Black folk? But there is always a conspiracy against Black folk, right? Killing us didn't start yesterday. Think about this, we are ALL BREONNA TAYLOR, Bro! All the cracker cops have to do is run up in your house blasting their firepower, kill you in your sleep, and then chuck deuces and say 'my bad, wrong address.'"

"And nobody goes to jail." I'm pushing my couch up against the door at night, I'm so scared. Do you even realize the precedent set by this action? They can kill us for waking up Black. They can kill us for walking down the street Black. They can kill us sitting in our car with our family for possessing Black skin. They can even kill us for walking to the store to buy skittles. And you of all people know the value of skittles."

"And now they killing us in our sleep. So what happens when nobody Black is around with a cell phone to record their ass? And how many of us are being killed and the white media propaganda machine just decides not to inform the nation?"

"We inside and we outside getting killed and you walking around letting bitches pee in your beard. It is pee my brother, it is pee. So how's life being married to a bag of skittles?"

"Good man."

"Bro, you crossed over to the other side. The skittles got'em! The quickest way to take the fight out of a Black man is to give him some white pussy."

Sadikki clapped his hands loudly and spent around in his chair.

"You walked into the light! You were supposed to hit it and quit it, not hit it and fall asleep in it. The revolution is about to start and you on the other side pointing a gun at us to protect the slave master's daughter."

He covered his face with his hands and shook his head.

KayBee answered proudly, as though he'd rehearsed the words many times before.

"Love does not have a color, number one. And number two, there will never be a revolution, so I have nothing to worry about."

"What side would you choose?" Sadikki asked.

"What do you mean?" KayBee asked while getting heated at the friend he'd met at Jake Gaither Gymnasium while working out. At the time, Sadikki was on the wrestling team. Both having a love for sports, they became friends, and kept in touch over the years. It was just pure coincidence that another brother from FAMU had relocated to Charlotte, North Carolina as well.

"Us or her?" Sadikki asked, still possessing sinister thoughts.

"My wife?" KayBee asked for clarity, steam rising from off his shoulders.

"Your wife or your race?"

Kavonnie jumped up and looked around quickly, making sure the coast was clear on the corporate plantation. Overseers lurked often. His breathing got heavier, chest rising and falling faster and his vision turned red. He opened his mouth to reply but nothing came out. He cleared his throat but before he could open his mouth a second time, Sadikki interjected.

"All I'm saying is that it is a strange time to be Black. So strange in fact, more Black men need to be standing by the Black woman's side; as husbands, as boyfriends, as family, and as protectors."

KayBee tried to calm his anger.

"We can't even protect ourselves as Black men. What the fuck I look like standing next to a Black woman that I'd have to watch get her ass kicked with me?"

Realizing the change in tone from a man that he considered a friend, Sadikki stood up slowly, maintaining eye contact with KayBee.

"I'm not trying to hate on your love for something white, I'm just really trying to express myself and illustrate my love for all things Black. Do you even remember the Florida Agricultural and Mechanical University motto?" He gave a pause, then said, "Black on Black everything, didn't stop just because we graduated."

"I love my wife," KayBee said. "Don't ever fucking question that or where I stand with my own race."

Then, he turned around and left.

As soon as he got outside, KayBee took a deep breath. He ordered a Lyft to head back to his office. In his mind, Sadikki's voice reverberated "*P-T-S-S...Post Traumatic Slave Syndrome.*"

"Nah, it's bullshit. That nigga lying" KayBee thought. "He's trying to conduct calisthenics inside my head."

After a conversation with himself, he made up his mind that his friend with the equally tight beard had to be simply delusional. After all, he was married to a white woman. So what did that mean? Was he asymptomatic to the disorder?

Your wife or your race?

KayBee didn't love his wife because she was white. He just loved her, all of her, including the skin that covered her. Hell, he could've ended up marrying a Black woman, things just never worked out with them.

Kavonnie met his wife in a dual enrollment Statistics class that he took at Florida State University. Although his major enrollment was at FAMU, there were certain classes that both schools allowed you to take at either campus. Since that class, he had never left Oliviann's side. He was faithful to his wife but felt the need to act like he had a side piece so that his FAMU brothers wouldn't think he was overly committed to the white folk. He wanted to maintain the authenticity of his Blackness at all cost. And what better way to exemplify being a Black man, than to act like you cheat on your wife. *Bro you crossed over to the other side. The skittles got'em!* Sadikki's voice kept resonating through his head.

He decided that he would replay the entire conversation to his wife. Her opinion was more important than Sadikki's or any other Black man. He was curious to hear what Oliviann would say about his friend's PTSS diagnosis. KayBee smiled at the idea of his wife's reaction. The white woman that he loved would decide how he should feel about the Black man that he allowed to roil his emotions.

8

....

TUESDAY WAS LUNCH with Dad.

He saw me before I saw him and called out to me.

"Hey son!"

"How'u doin' Pop?" I greeted my father with a smile.

"Glad to see your face because your face is my face too."

It was something my dad started saying a few years ago. I couldn't really argue because I did have the man's face; the younger version of course.

"I don't care what nobody says, and I don't care what nobody does." We chimed simultaneously.

"My life must be good..."

"If I look just like you!" We instantaneously continued laughing at the intimate rhyme we shared.

I sat down and took a sip from my coffee. Handing my father a cup of coffee as well, "Here you go Pop. It's nice and hot with your favorite Nutri Grain bagels in the bag."

I watched my family peak in the bag then with a sly smile look back at me.

"Whatcha thinking about?" I asked him.

"You're always on time and just in time. How is work?" My father asked.

"Before we get to that, for the one thousandth time." Hunching my shoulders with open palms in the air, "I have to say this, I have a beautiful bedroom with its own bathroom that's yours when you want it." Leaning over to give my dad a body bump, "You do know that I'm going to keep asking you, right?"

"I am one with nature and nature is one with me. I'm not lacking for anything and not everyone that is homeless is homeless."

My dad smiled and touched his head as if he had just expressed the greatest wisdom ever spoken.

"So life with my mother was really that bad?" I took another sip of coffee while awaiting his response.

"Life with your mother was never bad." He sipped his coffee and bit into a bagel, purchasing time to gather his thoughts.

I was sure he could feel my confusion. Energy on the verge of anger or maybe even the verge of breakdown; we both had to be careful. Our relationship was always a grenade without a safety pin. Possibly amenable in appearance but not the parental bond that one should have with their adult child.

"Marriage is beautiful and your mother was beautiful, up until the day that life left her hand in mine. There was a tinge in the middle of my palm."

He held his eyes shut tight with his left palm to his nose and if searching for a smell. "That slight tinge was her spirit leaving, her last tickle for me. I knew then without opening my eyes that she was gone. Gone and never to be replaced. I sit here before you still never having touched, in mind or body, the skin of another woman."

My father is purple Black with big, white eyes. When he uses his eyes to focus and make a point, they appear as if they just might fall out. His skin is smooth, and when his mouth is closed, it can be very hard to read him. I watched his eyes. That was where he hid or revealed his emotions. As I looked at him, I believed he was telling the truth.

"But she caged me. I tell you this all the time. Marriage will cage you. I was a lion of the jungle. Not in a sense of conquering women. I never held a mind to lust for every pair of panties walking in high heels. I only wanted two things in my life, to spend time with nature, nature was my first love before your mother. And like my father, secondly was to provide for my family. I grew up running through the forest of Mississippi, no specific city, all of it. I loved all of it. I fished every river. I fished every lake. Every land that allowed hunting in the entire state, I hunted and I conquered. Squirrel, deer, snake, and even the purest honey that bees could make. I love everything about nature. I was a lion of my jungle. I'm a country boy that fell in love with a city girl, and for a city girl, country living was shit. My first love was shit to her, as if it was a previous girlfriend that made her jealous."

"We didn't fuss and cuss about me being out late with the fellas, and no other woman ever called the house creating drama. We fought about my want to go be alive outside the city in my own comfort zone. But your mother wanted my comfort zone to be wherever she stood, and she stood in downtown; the very heart of the city. Concrete everything. No grass and no trees. You couldn't pay that woman to go into the woods."

He laughed and shook his head.

I sipped my coffee, feeling melancholy. Then, I recited a poem that instantly came to me:

"The older I get the more questions I have about yesterday,
even though yesterday seems so far away.
I might have spite,
I want tomorrow not yesterday, get out of my sight,
I bought a ticket to get away from yesterday and I thought I won the fight.
but there go yesterday sitting right next to me on the same damn flight.
Trying to escape my past,
I keep landing on my ass.
I wake up feeling blue in deep sorrow,
I can't wait 'til yesterday become friends with my tomorrow."

47

Dad finished his bagel and rocked back and forth. He swallowed the last bite and took a quick sip of his coffee, then wiped his mouth on his sleeve.

"Oh my, who's that one son?"

"I can't remember. I read too many books without memorizing the names on the spines; maybe Iceberg Slim or Donald Goines. Whoever wrote it, wrote it in jail, laying on a bunk trying to remember how he got there so he wouldn't end up back there; fighting his yesterday that got him locked up. So that his hope for tomorrow held freedom, or a sense of being closer to something that resembled freedom. Freedom can be confusing if you never actually tasted it."

"Well this is my freedom," Dad said. "And nothing happened yesterday that would scare me about what's coming tomorrow. Homelessness allows you to control your destiny."

He waved a finger to no one specific.

"The secret is living without a clock!" He tapped his head.

I questioned if anything was in there.

"I get confused sleeping with married women," I told him. "There's this sense of comfort that scares me because no matter what we do I know she is going to leave me, and I'm happy about that. I have these moments when I'm so happy being by myself with myself that I get scared that I'm going to end up like you."

I didn't want to look at him, so I kept my eyes focused forward; on the passenger doors of passing vehicles or the mail slot in the door of the business across the street when vehicles decided not to pass in front of me.

"I don't follow." My dad leaned back and blinked several times as if he didn't recognize his only son. "Who the hell told you that I was lonely?"

"You can be by yourself and lonely because you feel lacking. You feel like you need someone else to feel whole. What I'm telling you is that I feel whole most when I'm alone. I only want the temporary pleasure of another human being. I don't want a woman moving in with me. Or making me feel obligated. Or, as you would say, caging my inner lion. And I blame you for this feeling! It's not normal."

My father laughed loudly. He shook his head and waved his favorite finger again.

"Oh no, you and I are not in the same dimension. Not even close."

"Dimension? Really?" I rolled my eyes.

"These married women have placed your head, your heart and your penis in a blender and got you all discombobulated. You're a *ManBoy*! Running around here looking like a man, but when I measure your maturity, you're still a BOY! Just wait until the day comes that you get married. Sitting here judging your mother and I. You're getting older not younger. Stop using my marriage as a scapegoat and grow up. What are you afraid of?"

The look on his face is one of utter disgust, as if I fucked his child-hood up and not vice versa.

"Dad, you're not listening to me. I'm afraid to get married because I grew up in a house with a married couple."

"What the SHIT!"

"You and mom confused me." I finished my coffee, and placed my empty cup on the ground. "As a matter of fact, I have a very specific memory, you two confused me on that I think about on more occasions than I want to admit."

"Let me tell you what I remember." Dad delivered a dramatic pause, going almost catatonic.

He was the best at this. I was still perfecting me. I loved when he did this and couldn't help but smile.

He's utterly frozen from the tip of his big toe to that one strand of hair that continues to grow at the very top of his head and don't give a damn about the other millions of hair follicles that evacuated his scalp two decades ago. I really do practice this. There is something artistic about this gift. He's letting the entire world know that when he is ready, and only when he is ready, he is about to drop some shit on your ass to ponder forever and ever. His chest rises and falls. Here it comes! "I remember the day that I met your mother and every moment in between. Her life at meeting me to the day of her death. Our first date. Your birth. Our happy was our happy. But marriage is work. And so we worked. There is nothing that lasts from play only. You have to work as hard as you would like to play."

"I too remember." I reached over to squeeze my dad's shoulder.

"I remember you beating my mother in front of me. I remember you beat her unconscious. You stood over her limp and bloody body and just stared at her for a long time. I was crying of course. I screamed for you to stop but I knew you couldn't hear me. And I was much too afraid to get in front of your fist once you started swinging. I still have a wire in my jaw from making that mistake a few years later."

I touched my face for a short moment before continuing.

"But like something out of a cartoon or horror movie. I could never figure out if it was funny, scary or both. But you walked over to me, sat down and stared at your hands as if they weren't yours. It was as if you were confused on where the blood came from.

And after staring at your hands for a long time, you started clapping and looked at me and said, *"Did I ever tell you my secret for frying catfish? It's a family secret so you can't be running around sharing this with anyone and I mean anyone. Male or female, they can all go to hell. No one gets the family catfish secret. From the moment you pull that fish out of the water, and it must be nature fresh, don't you buy no catfish from no sto'."*

"And on and on you went about cooking this damn fish. But even crazier than that, my mom started coughing, but you were right in my face so I was scared to leave your gaze and give her any attention. But I could hear her coughing as she came to. She worked her way to her feet and limped over to the kitchen sink to splash her face with water. Next thing you know she says, *"How you gon' run your mouth about some catfish and you ain't cooking while ya' yapping. I'mma run down to the Korean Seafood Market and get some catfish. You's gone have to cook now that you's don' brought it up. I can't listen to this without my mouth salivating like a trained Pavlovian puppy."*

"Then you started laughing and said, *"Well go get it baby, AND MAKE SURE IT'S FRESH! I held my head in my hands and shook it from disbelief. Two hours later we are sitting at the kitchen table eating family secret ingredient covered catfish with macaroni and collard greens."*

"Like nothing ever happened. But the entire time I'm looking at both of you trying to figure out who's crazier. You for being you or her for being her, but you want to tell me how beautiful marriage is!"

I stopped him before he could interject.

"Dad, I'm not married because I grew up in a dysfunctional home that, today, has me loving dysfunctional. I don't want what you had if that's marriage."

"But it wasn't Son." I stare at him, wondering if he heard me or was he just waiting to speak.

"Our marriage was a lot of things but it wasn't anything like crazy or weird or out of the ordinary. You can choose any superlative you desire, but if you took all your descriptions of what we had and melted them all in a pot, the end result would be a stew called love."

Emotionally drained at this point, I screamed at my father, "We went from being on different dimensions to love stew, and you can't figure out why I'm fucked!"

"You can say whatever you want, but it wasn't that. I won't accept that. Love isn't always pretty or perfect or well-dressed or even well spoken. Sometimes it is downright ugly to the person looking in."

His eyes searched me for understanding.

"No matter what you saw, we represented love in everything that we did."

His left hand grasped an imaginary gavel and he slammed it down with the effect of reverberating a tangible noise. Although I watched his hand, I heard the finality in his voice. I closed my eyes at the sound of the invisible gavel and I kept them closed. Like a child again, I feared he might throw the imaginary gavel at me.

"I was in the sixth grade and I came home from school to you and mom having sex in the living room. You knew what time I would be walking in and you didn't care. You had to have heard my key in the door but you didn't stop. My presence didn't matter. And you know what I did after staring at the two of you panting and grunting like starved wolves in some Antarctic forest?"

Dad wouldn't look at me.

"I went to the kitchen and made a bowl of cereal and sat at the kitchen table. I got the loudest cereal we had and I stuffed my mouth to chew as loud as I could and I got no response from either one of you. You were right there on the couch. Maybe fifteen feet from me, and I know damn well you saw me."

Now I didn't want to look at him.

"I could never figure out what was worse. The erratic fighting, the erratic fucking or the walking through the house and not acknowledging each other's presence? My acknowledgement stopped years before you did it to each other."

"Are you blaming me for something? Are you blaming your mother for something? Because the last time I checked...."

He leaned in closer to me.

"The last time I checked her grave is that way. So why don't you write down all of your complaints and deliver them to the cemetery's management."

His ego gave me two stiff slaps on the back, while he wiped his hands in my face to signify his washing himself clean of our conversation.

"Stop blaming me for your personal bullshit. You're not a child. How can you just make this up and throw it in my face? Me beating your mother. Us having sex in front of you. Get the fuck out of here. That never happened!"

I hated crying in front of my father.

"You know dad it must be nice to live long enough to have such a privilege. I really hope that I live long enough to enjoy what you have."

He puts up his hands to imitate boxing.

"What's the punchline? I know it's coming. I see the tears. First tears then sarcasm."

My father also hid his emotions behind comedy, another inheritance.

"The privilege of forgetting. It must be nice to turn sixty-four and then decide not to remember the worst parts about yourself. The part of you that broke my mother and abused me. I really hope I live long enough to enjoy such a privilege. I think my generation would take less opioids and see less shrinks if we could just not remember shit like our parents. Even though it was our parents that did the shit that we most want to forget. The catalyst for our need for pills and our need to be heard. Our need to just escape somewhere that won't allow us to hear the fighting or fucking."

He dropped his boxer gloves and smiled.

I almost thought I saw a tear forming in one of his eyes. Almost. I stood up to walk away, sniffling.

"I really wish that we did live together. I have that room whenever you're ready. We may not always agree or even agree to disagree, but I do love you. I was too angry at mom to tell her before she died and I don't want to make the same mistake with you."

My father repeated a verse from the poem I had spoken earlier.

"I wake up feeling blue in deep sorrow, I can't wait 'til yesterday become friends with my tomorrow. Well I don't want yesterday to be friends with tomorrow. I want yesterday to stay yesterday, so that I DON'T remember a motherfucking thing when I wake up EVERYDAY! Every man in our family has suffered from Alzheimer's. I really wish I had a bottle of that shit right now. I throw a memory in the trash and then you go dig it out and give it back to me. All these questions and memories that you have are MEANINGLESS!"

He laughed loudly.

"Even if I tried to answer any of your questions, I'm only half the answer. What you don't realize is that your mother is the other half."

He hunched his shoulders.

"She's dead and dead don't answer questions, son."

There was that fatherly wisdom. *Dead don't answer questions.*

I was sure I'd marinate on that one forever.

"I love you dad."

I walked away, without waiting for a response.

As a child, I always felt like just maybe I was an accident. Maybe the pill hadn't worked, or my mom hadn't swallowed. My parents were always too busy with their shenanigans to realize that a child was watching. A child was in the room listening, a child that one day would no longer be a child anymore. If we all acted out what we saw our parents do, why in the hell would anyone ever get married?

I thought I heard my father screaming "son" in the background, or maybe it's what I wanted to hear; him actually begging or needing me, even if it was only temporary.

9

·················

I MET WITH the corporate crew every Wednesday at a bar called the *Bowden Ballers*. It's like a W.E.B. Dubois' mating ground for his Talented Tenth of the current era. Black, corporate shot callers from all the major firms. None of us own anything but our titles. But we could never lose our education and walls of degrees and certifications. Anything less than two degrees, you might not get in.

It is a beautiful space for the young, gifted and Black with live music, good food, overpriced drinks and a lot of women. Women of all colors came here. It didn't matter how Black an event may be, or where we decided to hang out as a people, you will not stop white women from attending. They always found or made a way to join us.

The spot has four private glass rooms with conference tables. We have the smaller room locked down for our weekly gatherings. It's VIP with privacy when we want it. When we closed the glass door, we could still enjoy the vibe of the space without the music drowning out our conversation.

We also had a private server who kept the bottles and food coming.

I dapped up half the crowd and made my way to our room. Greek was there. He got that nickname because he never stopped talking about frat life; the good ole days before he had to grow up. Greek was a stock broker, and one of the shortest in our crew. He was five-foot-four with no shoes, had a burnt pecan skin complexion and laughed much louder than a man that short should. He used to want us to call him the 'Purple Prince' in recognition of one of the colors of his fraternity, but we never did.

Big Brains walked in as soon as I sat down. The brother graduated college at age twelve and got two PhDs by sixteen. He was crazy awkward for the first two years, but we didn't give up on him. He was beyond smart and had a good heart. There was nothing that he couldn't figure out–except women. No man was that smart. Big Brains was the Chief Officer of Innovations and had over 400 patents. He was five-foot-nine but his confidence makes him appear a lot taller. He kept a short afro and represented Ghana to the fullest. He only wore suits and was always photo-shoot ready.

KayBee was the Corporate Banker who paid me a visit to my office earlier in the week. And then there was the attorney, my main man, Nice Head. We call him that because of his reputation with the women, meaning his tongue is best feature – according to the ladies. Nice head was five-foot-ten and although he maintained an athletic physique, none of us came close to KayBee in the muscles department. And then there is Silent Saint, a very spiritual brother who can hit you with a biblical scripture but not in an overly religious manner and make you feel good about it. He is very quiet and overthinks everything. He has a receding hairline that makes him appear older, but he never drinks beer or liquor and if any of us over do it, we can always count on him to get us home; Silent Saint is the Director of Marketing and an Assistant Pastor at his church.

In the crew I'm known as Knowledge – because even though I'm not as smart as Big Brains, I loved to read and debate. I was the tallest in the group, at six-foot-one, and my skin color was somewhere between Big Brains and Nice Head. On the plantation I act in the capacity of Assistant Director of Human Resources. We talk about life, work and women, of course, but we also discussed the state of Black America and ways we could improve our communities.

We all dapped up and ordered the first two rounds of drinks; shots to set the mood with a drink to chase the first shot to the head. We always started with one of every appetizer on the menu. We left the door open to enjoy the music, the ambiance and the eye candy. Having a room equates to status; at four hundred an hour plus food and drinks, the women knew what was up. One by one they lined up against the wall, staring and waiting to be selected. The bold ones tapped on the door and asked if they could join us.

For the guys, this was their only time away from wifey and the kids. I was the only single one, but this was the only day of the week when we all could hang out like this. Having substantial conversations with educated Black men meant everything to me, and the women were an added bonus.

I asked the server to close the glass door on her way out and then stood and tapped a spoon against an empty shot glass.

"Brothers let the conversation begin if you will. I've been waiting on this day to discuss a bitch ass Negro by the name of Mr. Lonnie Lamour. Who called a meeting of executives to inform us that Wellington and Wellington would be conducting an audit, and could we make sure not to fry chicken in the lunchroom during their visit."

Each brother gave out a loud expletive:

Greek was the loudest. "Get the FUCK OUTTA HERE! He didn't say that, you're a lying ass!"

Nice Head was rubbed his chin. "Dude is Black and he talks to ya'll worse than the SLAVE MASTER HIMSELF! That's CRAZY!"

"Oh yeah, that's a bitch ass fo' real," KayBee chimed in. "I don't even know why y'all acting surprised. Even billionaires are not free in this country, not the Black ones anyway; all the money in the world and he still waking up Black."

Big Brains had reviewed a list of multiple-choice questions in his mind but only shared one. "I'm going to go with answer C," he said, "As in I believe you're making this up. I've met him and there was no sign of self-hatred."

I pointed to Big Brains, "But when has self-hatred ever been blatant? And what's the point of being a Black billionaire if you sub-jugate your own people to the same silliness as the white folk?"

Greek finished another drink and said, "He's a Clarence Thomas and he's worse than the slave master. This man is an Overseer. Playing mind games to think he is dishing out brotherly love, but it's just another plantation. Maybe Black owned but still a planta-tion nonetheless."

"I don't know," Nice Head commented. "The white folk possess a skin privilege that no amount of money will ever hide for us. Maybe even Mr. Lamour is disappointed with what he still has to put up with but who's to say."

He looked around as if needing someone to affirm his statement.

KayBee shook his head, disappointed, "So money is not the answer to freedom then."

"Money has a very specific purpose," Big Brains spoke in a phil-osophical tone that only he possessed. "One should never connect currency to a principal or value such as freedom. You must control your inner-Nigga, you're speaking such foolishness. Freedom is freedom. Money is money. Never place them in the same category."

KayBee waved his hands for attention so no one could interject. "Hear me out Big B. That Black man is a billionaire who recruited thousands of other Blacks to work at companies he owns for a very 'specific type of freedom.' The freedom of not worrying about offending a lighter pigment with your Black. The freedom of not worrying about your name being too Black or not white enough; he will hire his own. The freedom to embrace and be embraced by the melanin culture."

He pointed to me.

"Now our brother just told you that Mr. Lamour called a meeting and spoke out loud, don't fry no fucking chicken because the colo-nizers are coming! Come on Bro, the man is denying freedom and at the same time selling freedom to his own people on a daily basis. So to connect the money or his billions, what I'm saying is, how could he get so rich and still be so dumb and untrustworthy? He's recruiting on the basis of freedom and denying freedom at the same time for the sake of what?"

He looked around at all of us.

"Somebody help me out please."

I cleared my throat and began, "And speaking of controlling my inner-Nigga, Mr. Brains you gotta look at it like this." Jabbing my chest, "I know how I felt hearing him speak that 'Mo' Tea Sir' fuckery. And I saw the pain in everyone's eyes. It wasn't funny, it was weak. And it was scary because we all look at him as the epitome of what we all can become. And to sit in such a position of comfort and power and be shaken by the arrival of the third kind is just disheartening. What's the purpose of becoming a billionaire if you can't find comfort in just being you? At what point can a Black man have enough money that he can just be Black? Can he take care of his own people without the Hollywood shuffle or church chicken dancing to appease the Euros?"

"I understand and overstand you both," Big Brains acknowledged Kaybee and then me. "You made a decision to place expectations on this man that he knows nothing about. Who told you," he pointed back and forth at KayBee and myself, "that man achieved freedom? No one. You simply assumed that his money gave him favor with the non-melanated. But my question is why? Black poor and Black rich are the same in Ameri-can't. You're speaking like he escaped to Haiti; an island of true revolutionaries. But it wasn't no escape. That man still right here in a country with government agencies that exist every day to ensure his and our captivity or death. So in my opinion, you both are asking the wrong questions. Ameri-can't answers every Black man's questions that decide to live in this country. That answer to every question is white. Not right, but white. So let me ask all of you, why would you become a billionaire and stay in Ameri-can't?"

"Because it's our country too and it was our country first," Nice Head said with authority. "There is no such thing as an Indian. Those were Africans but that white man ain't stupid. Divide the people, okay we gon' call these darkies Indians and we gon' call these darkies African and we know these darkies are truly African because we paid their cruise fair to get here. But at some point in the future, these dumb ass niggas ain't gon' stay dumb, and since we are only allowing a small population to be called Indian, we will only have to give reparations to the 'small portion of them' and not all of them. We'll let the other darkies just keep crying foul. And that's what we have been doing since 1865, screaming foul and WE AIN'T LEAVING!"

I tried to stifle my laughter as I jumped up as several brothers started speaking simultaneously.

"But wait a minute," I said. "Wait a minute. Let's go back to Brains. We are all smart men. And you all have extremely smart wives. I have no idea why they married any of you, but they are smart nonetheless. Now here's my question; why are any of us still in Ameri-can't? Why are any of us still on the plantation? We don't have to be billionaires to leave. So why are any of us still here?"

The server came in and interrupted the debate.

She said, "Y'all look way too serious in here. I'mma leave the door open because there is a party out there in case you forgot."

She beamed an irresistible smile and began to take individual orders.

Ninety minutes later, after the musician's first set, the glass door was closed and we were all laughing and pontificating without talking.

Greek told the same damn story he always told, about being on line pledging, and how hard it was but how thankful he is because his line brothers still take care of him to this day. Big Brains talked about a new virtual reality invention and asked if any of us wanted to volunteer to play with the proto-type and then fill out a survey for his research firm. KayBee discussed the details of a deal that he was trying to close, and Nice Head was in the middle of one of his freaky stories about how he was going down on a set of twins when one almost shit in his face.

Everyone was laughing and slapping the table when I noticed Silent Saint standing at the closed, glass door. I looked in his eyes and stopped laughing immediately. I stood up and walked toward the door.

One by one, each brother became silent and stood as we noticed the pain on Silent Saint's face. He was a quiet and humble man, but never sad or numb. I opened the door and moved to the side so that he could walk by. He held his head down and walked slower than normal.

KayBee barked out a loud, "Yo! Where the fuck are your dreads man?"

I turned quickly and motioned with my head side-to-side that this was not a joking moment. Our spiritual brother's spirit was damaged. I looked at each man sitting and standing and waved for them to come closer. I wrapped my arms around Silent Saint and the other brothers joined us.

And there we were, the six of us, trying to pour our love into one amongst us who was evidently in agony.

Silent Saint jerked his body and said, "I'm good. I'm good. Thank you all but I'm good."

We stepped back to give him space but Big Brains, who was a lot taller, stayed near with a hand on one of his shoulders.

Big Brains pushed him ever so slightly but never actually letting go of his shoulder, "Just let us know what happened. You can start talking whenever you're ready. We are all right here with you Bro."

Hyped from the liquor, Greek did something with his legs and hands and yelled when he meant to just talk, "TAKE YOUR TIME JESUS! WE GOT YOU!"

Silent Saint shook his head and moved to sit down. He asked for some water, which I was already pouring him. He gulped his water and opened his mouth to speak.

"I love my church but I don't always understand the people in it. The elders of the church called me in two days ago. They sat me down with these two clowns, you know, some white boys, jumping up and down, talking fast. It all sounded like jibber jabber until they stopped and were just looking at me. I mean I was listening, not listening. After all these years, there was a part of me thinking, are they going to fire me? I mean I can't believe how frightened I was. But then I realized that I wasn't scared. It was more of a premonition that something really bad or sad was about to happen and I was going to have to make a decision."

"So what were they talking about?" I inquired.

"Well it seems that Mecklenburg Methodist wanted me to take a new assignment within the church leadership but with a catch."

Nice Head's speech was extremely slurred, but we all understood him clearly, "They made you cut your hair! Your dreads! Your strength!"

Silent Saint rubbed his head as Nice Head spoke.

"These two white boys said that my hair may offend some of our higher net worth congregants. And if I wanted to be a team player and be given the opportunity to utilize my full potential at the church, they ASKED ME, if I would consider cutting my dreads off because they wanted me to become a symbol for all believers. The funny thing is my bishop never spoke. He just sat back and observed this circus. Every now and then he would just stare at me but he never uttered a word. And these two guys! I'm not even sure that I've ever seen them at the church before."

"Give us an example of what they were saying and speak verbatim," Big Brains commanded.

At this point Saint was crying. Tears ran down his face in a pattern similar to his lost dreads as if mourning their disappearance.

"Once they asked me to cut my hair, I was no longer coherent. They kept repeating *'This isn't racism....... we believe in the power of diversity... and God doesn't see color.... And we don't want you thinking about discrimination. Do not allow the devil to enter your mind. No one is even thinking about color. This isn't about color. It's about a future, your future standing in the church. We want to elevate you Pastor Saintinus. We just need you to present a cleaner look that emblazons the founding name and culture of this church and Christianity. We need people to meet you and feel blessed by your presence and not think Busta Rhymes or Lil Wayne. I'm sure you can understand that.'"*

Nice Head seemed to have regained clarity, "Wait a minute. That was racist as fuck!"

We all shouted in agreement.

"I know you don't curse," Nice Head continued, "So I'm saying it for you. Did they give you a contract to sign for this shit? FUCK THAT, DON'T SIGN SHIT WITHOUT ME READING IT! I WANNA READ THAT SHIT!"

Saint whispered something quietly through his tears. I looked around at the others because I thought I heard him, but didn't like what I heard. He grabbed his head with his hands as if he was trying to tear off his own scalp, and began shouting.

"MY CONTRACT IS WITH GOD! I SIGNED A CONTRACT WITH GOD AND CUT MY HAIR FOR....! I CUT MY HAIR FOR..... GOD!"

Saint sounded as if he was trying to convince himself. Big Brains was the closest and grabbed him.

Again the brothers gathered around Silent Saint with love and support through a group hug. We shared words of support, of encouragement, to uplift and push past with a goal of helping him regain his inner strength. The server creeped in slowly and asked if we needed anything.

To the surprise of everyone, Silent Saint turned in his seat to face the server and asked for double shot of Tequila.

We were all too stunned to speak.

The server looked at me and I shook my head side-to-side and mouthed the word 'Water.'

She nodded her understanding and removed Kaybee and Nice Head's empty plates.

Big Brains stood behind Silent Saint in deep and quiet thought.

I heard drums and applause and the vibe outside seemed like a great way to change the energy in the room. Kaybee must have sensed it also because after the server left, he kept the glass door open to air out all of the heated tension of Silent Saint's situation.

And if that wasn't enough to change the mood, without any notice, a very sensuous, white woman walked into our room. She held her head high, shoulders back, possessed with all the confidence of an African, Zulu Queen.

Nice Head, beaming with all his white teeth showing, completed a dance move and slid left to block her path. The woman did a two-step to the right, and walked past him without smiling.

Everyone's eyes were on her – or some part of her legs, breast, lips. She stopped in front of me, held up her purse and then pulled out a small bag of skittles with her name in black marker on one side and her phone number on the other. She opened my suit jacket, slid the skittles inside my inner pocket and kissed my right cheek.

She looked in my eyes and said, "There's more where that came from."

She didn't even wait for me to respond. She turned and walked out the same way that she walked in, but this time she patted Nice Head on the head on her way out.

Feeling some kind of way, he yelled after her, "I'm not that short. HELL NAW! I'm not that SHORT!"

We all laughed and it really felt good to see Silent Saint laughing as well. And just like that, side conversations began between two brothers to my right and two brothers to my left, and Nice Head somewhere in the crowd dancing to the beat.

I sat back amazed that in this moment of time and post-Obama presidency, Black people still don't truly enjoy the freedom that comes with American citizenship. The very idea that a Black man or woman's hair can offend a member of the white race is simply repulsive to our very existence. Once of the privileges of being in the melanated club is that we possess hair that no other race can enjoy. But corporate demands are corporate demands and they are always demanding of us to be like them. Act white like them. Look white like them. Dress white like them. Sound white like them because anything else is not fitting of the organizational culture and comfort of your White peers. How is it a burden simply looking at our Black hair of any style? So much pain we cause the Europeans.

I walked over and closed the glass door to deaden the music. Simultaneously the brothers started yelling at me to not kill the mood and let Silent Saint be. I raised my hands to silence everyone.

I pulled a chair and sat in front of Silent Saint

"I'm sorry brother," I said, "But I love you and I need you to share with me the scripture you gave yourself pertaining to this situation? Here we are again dealing with some White supremacy, Corporate nonsense that is flat out demeaning and racist. Give me something please because I'm trying to picture myself in your situation and all I see is me going Silverback ape shit. How did you get out of that room without killing anyone?"

The Black Pastor is an exquisite actor. He always knew when he had his audience's attention; when to pause, speed up, or be silent, loud, dramatic, or humble.

I think of all of this as Silent Saint sat there manipulating time and our emotions. We are holding on to every movement of his chest, watching the air enter and exit, waiting on that air to hold words with the keys to free us from chains of impatience.

"Speak Silent Saint. Please speak."

He rubbed his chin, and blinked sporadically as if he can see his bible just in the distance but not close enough that he can read the words.

"Speak Silent Saint speak. Give us something."

He looked around at us and spoke calmly.

"Luke 23:24; Love them anyway."

We stood simultaneously, and embraced for the third time.

"Thank you," I shook his hand.

I was fucking disgusted. I opened the glass door and left. My mind was flooding with rebuttals to his biblical fuckery.

Once again, the Black man had to humble himself and pray for his enemy after his enemy with a wide smile slapped one cheek and then the other, because he knew that's how the Black man has been trained. Once again, the Black man had to be the humane one in an act of inhumanity against his very existence. I didn't want to pray for my enemy or forgive my enemy, I wanted to kill him.

But since I couldn't fight the entire white world, I could at least go fuck a slave master's daughter. I moved through the crowd searching for the Casper that gave me the skittles.

10

....

RECOMMENDATIONS WERE REQUIRED for reprimanding or firing. I sat in my office, reading profiles of several employees. The company really did try to work with people, but some behaviors were so blatantly unprofessional that they were downright scary. I knew that I was dealing with people's lives, but my job was to preserve company culture, not help an idiot, with a wife and kids, keep his job. I was given a tremendous amount of freedom to utilize my own judgment.

I was just about to type notes when my secretary walked in.

"Just a reminder, you have Mr. JaJa at TopGolf at 2:00 pm. You told me to interrupt whatever you were doing and not to leave until I can walk out behind you."

I dropped my head and closed my eyes.

"I said that?"

"Yes Sir, you sure did, so let's go."

I laughed, saved my work and logged off the computer.

"Can you tell Mrs. Lava that I haven't made a decision on these files, and I won't be returning from this meeting?"

I grabbed my jacket and Khadijah followed behind me.

My meeting at TopGolf was with JaJa–another FAMU alumni. Another Brainiac who I competed with over grades when we had class together. I usually won with the exception of Corporate Finance. That was the first class that ever challenged me. JaJa breezed through it, and at the same time, saved my ass with tutoring.

The Lyft ride was short. I always arrived early to get in one round of putting, before JaJa got there. We were constantly competing and golf was another activity that he was naturally good at. I was on my last hole when I heard JaJa from behind.

"You can come early as many times as you want," he laughed. "And you're still getting your ass kicked."

I dropped my putter to embrace my friend.

"Appetizers and a bottle of Tequila are on the way." I told him.

"You know how we do." We said in unison, laughing "ALL NIGHT STUDY SHOTS !!!"

"I can never remember how that shit started, tequila shots and studying for an exam. FUCKING GENIUS! Who knew?" I shook my head.

"I remember clearly. It was that damn girl, Queefa. Remember, it was just the three of us. After the fourth shot, she acted like she was drunk and took off her clothes. Then she started grabbing on me and....." JaJa stopped speaking, yanked at his sports jacket and winked.

"No, no, no, no," I objected. "And HELL NAW !!! No way that woman grabbed you for anything if I'm in the room. She looked at you, and looked at me. Then, she started grabbing me, and your dumb ass was watching us until I grabbed her by the face with my dick up her ass and asked her if you could join us. I mean you were about to cry and shit."

"Oh yeah, she just gave me some head that night."

JaJa looked around and rubbed the back of his head, to wipe away the embarrassment.

"Oh yeah, and she gave me some of everything. I mean it took a while, but eventually I got her to give your weak ass some ass too. Bro you had zero game in college; I mean college of all places. It was the largest, designated free pussy zone on the planet. All you had to do was say hi to a girl, and she'd give you her panties. What the hell was wrong with YOU! A historically Black college where girls outnumbered the guys forty to one and you were walking with no squad. I got to FAMU and racked up a starting line-up, some bench players and then back up bench players. I wanted all forty of my girls on campus." I said indignantly.

"Yeah but all those girls created a problem." JaJa was looking at me closely for a response.

I shrugged my shoulders and steadied myself for my next swing. I swung and pulled left. Then winced as I watched my golf ball go straight then curve left and hit the fence.

"Come on bro," I said. "Anyone would lose focus getting that much ass. It was my first time on a college campus, number one. Number two, at FAMU there were sixty people in a class and fifty-four of those people were female. Number three, the school is located in Florida and it was a hundred degrees and the girls were coming to class half naked. Number four, I was the smartest person in damn near every class and number five, I look good. So yeah, only half the girls in every class wanted to sit on my dick or my face; pick your order. What was I supposed to do, scream STOP DISTRACTING ME WITH ALL THIS WETNESS!"

"Must have been nice." JaJa shook his head and stuffed his face.

After he finished eating, he took a shot and stood up to choose a putter.

"But you bounced back," he called over his shoulder.

Snoop Dogg is six-foot-five inches and weighs one-hundred and eighty pounds, which is ridiculously skinny for that height. My brother JaJa is a burnt carbon copy of the rapper. He was a dark-skinned brother with long legs and long arms, and he always walked slowly as if any speed might hurt him. He was a sharp dresser in college, and kept up his style after graduation. He also gave the best Snoop Dogg impression I've ever seen.

"Because of you brother, because of you. It should be illegal to have that much ass in one setting. I mean seriously, registering at FAMU should have come with some type of ass disclaimer."

I smiled at the thought.

JaJa swung and missed the golf ball entirely, laughing uncontrollably.

I don't know if my joke was that funny or the tequila was kicking-in. After he finally gathered himself, he swung and missed again. Then he straightened up, wound his arms in several circles each and reshuffled his feet.

JaJa spoke to the putter in his hands, "Come on baby." He swung again and missed his designated hole entirely and watched his ball fall into oblivion. He walked over and put his putter back in the holder.

"Let me sit my ass down because I'm starting to feel shot by tequila shots."

We joked around some more about college and then post college life. We laughed at how dreams don't always become reality, and all the things we would do differently if life had a do-over button.

Halfway through the bottle, I asked about work.

"So how is life on the corporate plantation? Is mergers and acquisitions everything you thought it would be?"

"Actually it's not bad. I mean, the white folks don't always share information with me, but I get around that the best way that I can," JaJa answered blandly.

I asked, "Is that white people being white people or is it a competitive environment that comes with interacting in that arena?"

"I think most white people are naturally good people. I would say it's competition and nothing else." JaJa answered.

"But if you're the only Negro in the room," I started. "Where's the competition? They hold all the cards and you're not sitting in any position of power. So why would anyone feel the need to keep information from you? Either they are not naturally good people or you did something to piss them off, like woke up Black!"

I rolled my shoulders because I could feel myself getting tense.

"No power yet, but it's coming. I just worked my way up two prongs on the ladder of success with my last power move." JaJa was school girl giddy.

Now something fell in my stomach.

"*POWER MOVE?*" I was in shock. "You made a power move. Your conservative, scary, Black ass did not make a power move Bro; details homey! Details! Cough it up on the table so I can analyze this shit."

JaJa laughed and took another shot.

"You ever hear of two companies, *Paradigm Shift* and *Momentum, Incorporated?*"

"Of course, two of the largest, Black owned corporations in Charlotte. We've done some light human resources training throughout the years at each one."

I enjoyed nice memories of the people at those companies.

"You pay attention to the news?" JaJa asked.

"I have to, there was a merger deal on the table that fell apart and just over eight hundred brothers and sisters lost their jobs when it didn't happen. We've been contracted to help the newly unemployed find jobs in Charlotte first of course, but a lot of the vacancies are in Durham and Raleigh. So more than likely, a lot of them will be relocating."

JaJa beat his chest then raised his hands in the air.

"That was me. I killed the deal. Power move! I was chosen to sit with the Board of Directors at each company and make an assessment on intellectual capacity, direction of the company, one, three, five and ten year goals. I looked at the feasibility of the merger, and didn't like what I saw. So I killed it."

"You are personally taking responsibility for the unemployment of eight hundred Black people?" I was stunned.

"I didn't like what I heard or saw." JaJa expected me to compliment him.

I was confused.

"Define what the fuck you heard and then define what the fuck you saw!"

"I can start by telling you what I didn't see."

JaJa stood in front of me with his hands on his hips.

I just stared at my FAMU brother, whose words became screeching sounds hurting my ears. The pride he took in what he believed to be an accomplishment was in opposition to the character I thought he possessed.

I dropped the putter from my hand so that I wouldn't use it on his face.

"We may fire people but it is never the first option my team chose. And if I were in a position to make a decision affecting the lives of so many people, I would have exhausted all means within my power to keep them employed. All of them!"

After I didn't reply, he finally leaned closer and said, "I didn't see anyone white on either board of directors. Not one fucking white person. How could any plan they have possibly be feasible or even profitable for that matter? Absent of white intellect, those companies were doomed by nature."

JaJa grinned, almost laughing.

"You." I said. "The man I consider a brother and a friend, think white people are smarter than Black people?" I was utterly devastated.

"I think white intellect is needed where Black intellect is concerned. You can have an all-white intellectual component absent of anyone Black, but I would advise against an all-Black component absent of anyone white. That's all I'm saying. Bill Gates is not Black and Steve Jobs is not Black. So what are we doing?"

I fell silent. I was in pain. My mind began racing in so many directions. I went to Egypt and immediately thought about the world's first university created by intellectual Black men who taught the Greeks. Only for the Greeks to come back and steal the knowledge and burn down the university; then lie to the world as if education started in Greece. I thought about the Bible being raped of its Black people, names changed from African, the book of Osiris, to something European, the book of Mark. The Bible got repackaged and white washed then given to Blacks to praise something that was originally theirs anyway. Blacks created everything, and yet I'm

72

sitting with a Black man who thinks otherwise. Ignorance is sheer whiteness and always has been; white folk just make good thieves.

JaJa paid the waitress and I came back to my present mind. I put my jacket on and waited for him. The world seemed fogged.

"You understand right." I saw the apprehension in his eyes.

He wanted my approval of the back-stabbing he had committed against his own people. Our people.

"What did the white folk give you for your *power move?*" I used finger quotes.

He smiled.

"I saved our company millions from a deal that would have eventually ended on a sour note. And for that, I got invited to the annual retreat in Bermuda."

He seemed proud of this achievement. His chest seemed fuller, even higher after speaking these words. He bent forward and added, "It's exclusive."

"No promotion and nothing monetary. Just a pat on the head and an invitation to play *Toby*." I dropped my head and began rubbing my face with both hands.

"You play token nigger until you get more tokens, NIGGA!" Now his face became hardened as he laser beamed me with his eyes.

"I apologize. I get confused. I actually think all Black people working in corporate America are on the same team. That we all have the same perspective; us against them. I always feel disheartened when I realize one of us actually believes he or she is one of them. You're on the wrong team Ja. Unity only works if we are all on the same side. Black on black everything, remember?"

"The white team is the winning side, and I chose the winning side as soon as I got the job. Fuck your Black unity. It doesn't exist, and it never will."

"Not when we have brothers like you, right?" I walked over to him and raised my hands.

He flinched as if expecting me to throw a punch.

"Calm down brother." I gently embraced his cheek with a hand then placed a hand on each of his shoulders. "To be violent is to be white. Please remember that. Black people are naturally accepting and forgiving. There will come a day that I will forgive you also, but before that day comes, I would like to share a story with you that I hope you'll remember."

"The Emancipation Proclamation took place September 22, 1862, freeing slaves. The confederacy didn't recognize this act, or claimed to not to know, until June 19, 1865; what we Black folk celebrate today as Juneteenth. There was a certain plantation right outside of what today is Denton, Texas where the slave master just didn't like ole' Nigger loving Abe Lincoln; after all, what kind of American't president would free niggers. It just didn't make sense to Mr. Wilkey Finch. Niggers were supposed to be the property of white folks for perpetuity. God created Blacks to be the slaves of Whites, and you just don't go messing with God's work."

I squeezed his shoulders.

"Anyway," I continued. "Mr. Finch had an albino slave named *Flour* because his skin was white as flour. The whites of the Finch family made fun of Flour and the slaves made fun of Flour; everyone made fun of him. Over the years he grew more and more intolerant of the slaves and all their jokes and put downs. Mind you that whites made fun of Mr. Flour as much, if not more so, but he didn't mind that because inside of his twisted and perverted mind, he sided with the whites. In his mind the only thing that gave him any sense of salvation was that his skin was closer to the color of massa' than it was the color of those godforsaken slaves. He wasn't Black is what he would tell himself. Even though he ate with the slaves. Even though he slept with the slaves. And even though he worked side-by-side with the slaves. He simply refused to believe that he was one of the slaves."

"The slaves had their own means of communicating scuttle-butt from plantation to plantation. And according to scuttle-butt, they's suppose'b free but massa won't let'em. You see it was September 1963, exactly one year since the '*emancipation proclamation*' and they were still slaves in the grand land of Texas. But they had heard of a brave, white man named Mr. Lincoln who proclaimed them free. And they wanted their freedom. Something needed to be done and there were several men on the plantation that wanted to revolt and kill ole' massa Finch. The slaves were determined to get what they deserved. Why not? They's American too! And the one thing all Americans fight for, is their freedom."

"When the day came and everyone was ready, to their surprise, when they came around the bend upon massa Finch's house, there he stood with the local militia on horseback and guns drawn. On that day 75 slaves were burned alive for having the audacity to believe that just because the president of their country said that they were free, that the Lord's good, southern white folk had to capitulate. So how did massa Finch know about the planned revolt? I'll tell you how Ja, his trusted slave, Flour, spilled the beans. And in return for stopping the revolt, Flour received a pat on the head and all the pancakes he could eat for a week."

I hugged my brother because I knew that it would be the last hug that I would ever give him and turned around. When I got to the door, I opened it with my right hand and turned to face him, pointing a finger of my left hand to his face.

"WHEN YOU GET TO BERMUDA, ENJOY THOSE PANCAKES MOTHERFUCKER! Self-hatred is one kind of demon, but to hate your entire race is something even more blasphemous. One day I'll forgive you, Ja. But right now, I have to remove myself from your presence, brother."

"YOU DON'T UNDERSTAND THE PRESSURE I WORK UNDER!" JaJa thundered.

"I got the same pressure, Ja. Every Black man in this country is born under the same pressure. Every Black woman born in this country is under the same pressure. You want to know what's really ironic?"

I took my right hand back and let the door close. "Black people are always talking about the plantation, the plantation, but the real plantation is this entire fucking country; ocean to ocean and northern border to southern border. American't. American't, Ja. AMERICA CANNOT LOVE BLACK PEOPLE but this country is extremely good at tearing us apart. You sat in my face and beat your chest after informing me that you're responsible for hundreds of Black men and women losing their jobs. Their homes destroyed. Their lives destroyed. Unity starts with us. You and me and then we add one, who adds one who adds one who adds one. We are BLACK FIRST! BLACK ON BLACK EVERYTHING!"

"They'll find another job and if they can't, then they deserved to be fired because of their limiting capabilities or allowing themselves to be short-sighted. Do you care about the people you fire Mr. Hypocrite?"

"GODDAMN you! Are those your words or the white folk that you work with? Who did you hear say that? Don't lie to me!" I found myself walking in small circles. I stopped and jabbed a finger in his direction, "I'm not a hypocrite. Firing people is never the first option unless they do something utterly ridiculous, create a hostile environment or actually touch someone else without their permission. It is NEVER the first solution if it can be avoided."

He turned away from me and swallowed hard.

"Enjoy your pancakes, Ja. Don't ever fucking call me again. I don't understand why did you go to FAMU and surrounded yourself with your own people if you hate us so much?"

"Because I couldn't get into Florida State University. My experience there was not like yours. I didn't get invited to all the parties. I didn't have a starting line-up of girls and a bench to choose from. I didn't get solicited to join fraternities. We may have both been nerds, but you were a nerd and cool. You were the life of the party but studied before going to the party. While I sat outside just wishing that I could get invited. The only time anyone was nice to me was when I was with you."

"I hated the loudness of Black people. Talking loud. Walking loud. Driving by in their cars with their loud, satanic music degrading our culture and our women. Loud bass, expletive, more bass, expletive. FAMU was a bunch of wannabe Black intellectuals that idealized the street culture in the hallways while imitating a caricature and articulation of corporate white folks in front of the class. We were no better than the Bethune Cookman students that we made fun of. So yeah, my hatred for Black people started on that historically piece of shit campus that you brag about."

JaJa shook his head at me.

"You're a sad man, JaJa. The white folk that you work with will never give you the respect that you're searching for. And those pancakes are going to be limited. Enjoy them while you can. Because once the pancakes stop coming, their expectations for you to produce will be even higher."

I headed for the exit a second time.

"You just don't.." JaJa started as I opened the door again.

"We all wake up Black, Ja." I cut him off. "We are all committing the same crime. Your pressure is my pressure. We have all been sentenced."

This time I allowed the door to close behind me.

I stood outside of Top Golf trying to decide what to do. Walk and think or a Lyft home. Before I could come to a decision, a co-worker that lives in my building saw me and asked if I wanted a ride. I nodded with a thin smile. I was able to avoid awkward chatter because he was on a date; allowing me continued contemplation of my conversation with JaJa.

I got home and went to get a bottle of Tequila for medication. I needed healing. I was still annoyed from JaJa's words. He intentionally killed a deal because the room was filled with Black people – his own people. Black people like him existed right under my nose. How many more graduated from FAMU like JaJa and hated the Black experience? How many more are at FAMU right now waking up every day wishing to be on a whiter campus?"

I don't believe in church because it's the white indoctrination center. If you want to make a nigger, send him to church. I don't believe in public education because it's the white indoctrination center. If you want to make a nigger, send him to public school. I don't believe in prison because it's the white indoctrination center, aka, the nigger factory. If you want to make a nigger, send him to prison. I don't stand for the national anthem because it is not for Black people. And I don't respect the flag of American't. Slaves may have sewn that flag, but it was never created to be flown above Black heads in a position of anything equal to anything white.

It is all WHITE FUCKERY! Someone white took something black and repackaged that shit and gave it back to Black people and said, look what I did. Our music, our religion, our culture, our inventions, our everything. American't was founded by immigrants. But it wasn't structurally created for the success of its Black inhabitants; immigrants or otherwise. Don't give your kids a name too Black, the white folk won't hire you. Don't dress too Black, the white folk won't feel comfortable. Don't talk too loud, the white folk will hear aggression. And smile more so the white folk won't fear you and shoot you. It is all WHITE FUCKERY!

And the worst white indoctrination center of them all is Corporate America. It causes Black men to turn on Black men under the guise of corporate competition. JaJa betrayed all of us, but I'm not naive to believe that he's the only one to commit such a heinous act against his own people. Supreme Court Thomas bitches existed way before JaJa. And Flour came even before Thomas's white massa loving ass. I really wish American't lived up to the values that it preached so that it could be the America we as Black people want. But it hasn't because American't.

I don't know when the tequila bottle became empty, or how I ended up on my living room floor. But I did know that I loved Black people. And that doesn't mean that I hate anyone else. And I wasn't like JaJa.

I tried to get up off the floor, but was unsuccessful. I grabbed a pillow from the couch to place under my head and continued to let my mind float on tequila clouds. The worst part of WHITE

FUCKERY is that indoctrinated Black folk divide Black people like white people divide Black people.

We forget about the first word and focus on the second. *'Black gay, oh no, that's an abomination in the bible, I can't mess with gay. Black-trans, oh no, he's confused. Look at the man in the dress, I can't mess with trans. Black Muslim, oh no, I was raised Baptist.'* Black and so what! Why can't Black people stay focused on the first word in the description, BLACK!

But we don't. And maybe that was the intent, but it wasn't actualized. We get indoctrinated and turn on each other. I couldn't believe what JaJa did. And it pained me more knowing that he took pride in the act, in exchange for a pat on the head and some fucking pancakes.

I needed more tequila. Tequila was the truth; it made us all tell the truth. I'm not indoctrinated DAMNIT! And I don't need tequila to help me say that. I'm not indoctrinated DAMNIT! I opened my eyes to the blue ceiling of my apartment. My mind showed me flashes of my life, from church, from public school, to conversations with relatives' fresh out of jail or prison, from college and then flashes from the corporate plantation. I began sweating and my chest heaved. OH SHIT! I HOPE I'M NOT INDOCTRINATED! I ran to the bathroom and put my head in the toilet. I wanted to vomit everything, especially the memory of losing one of my best friends.

I envisioned JaJa's face on top of everything that came out of my stomach, and had an epiphany. I saw his face swirling down the toilet, and into the sewer with all the other shit under the sidewalk, where we try to ignore it. White shit beneath our feet, ignore it. White shit in our faces, ignore it. White shit at work, ignore it. White shit at home, ignore it. White shit all around us that can't be ignored, and yet we keep screaming *'BLACK LIVES MATTER'* but how, if we only matter in a sewer of white shit!

11

BABA WAS SITTING in his office after everyone had left. He needed someone to speak to about his day, before discussing it with his wife when he arrived home. He walked outside into the courtyard with the perfectly manicured grass and took a seat on his favorite bench. He pulled out his cell phone to call Knowledge. "My brother, my brother. Do you have time to talk?"

When Big Brains called me, I could hear that something was very wrong.

"Are you still at work?" I asked.

"Yes I am," his voice was barely audible.

"No problem. I'm going to catch a Lyft to you, so go ahead and order us something to eat please. Whatever it costs, I'll cash app half of it back to you once I get there."

Once I got close to Brain's plantation, I sent a text. We greeted each other with smiles and a hug. I followed him out into a courtyard where bags of food sat on a bench. The bags read 'African Flavors' and I was not even surprised by his choice for a restaurant.

After we stuffed our faces, Big Brains asked me, "Do you think anything will change now that the George Floyd protests have happened?"

My mouth was still full, which gave me time to contemplate how I wanted to respond.

"No I don't actually. A lot of private corporations are screaming Black Lives Matter and adding words like inclusion, diversity, empathy and togetherness, but the top five lynchpins of the Black race have been as quiet as a white, church mouse. The Secretary of Education didn't say Black Lives Matter, so our children are still going to be fed a white-washed history lesson. The Secretary of Housing didn't say Black Lives Matter, so in order for the Black woman on section eight to receive any benefits, she is still going to have to deny the father of her children from living with his family. The Department of Justice didn't say Black Lives Matter, so Negroes will still be forced to take the plea bargain. Yeah nigger we know you're innocent but take the plea."

"This is a country that prides itself on giving the alleged a trial by jury, but nobody Black is getting a jury. Which means the DOJ will continue to pack us like sardines in prisons, to send us to work for the fortune five-hundred plantations in basements that people don't know about, and on chain-gangs that people think don't exist anymore but do. No one from the hospital industry said Black Lives Matter, so our people will continue to be victims of a medical apartheid. And last but never the least, Black Water Matters! Can the Negroes in Detroit please get some clean water? Hell nah nothing is changing, I'm even surprised that you would waste your time asking such a question. What's really on your mind Brains?"

Big Brain's voice sounded as stressed as it had been on the phone.

"I have always had an affinity for our conversations. I love it when we're all together but there is something special about being able to verbally joust like this with another brother."

I laughed.

"True dat and likewise," I agreed. "I can't really get this deep with the other brothers, and I think that it's funny when I compare and contrast my individual conversations with each one of you. Like you and I break bread over Black history, most of the time. Compare that to my conversations with KayBee, and they be ignorant as hell."

I continued laughing hoping to return to a lighter mood.

"Choosing FAMU was one thing," Big Brains started. "But meeting you guys was definitely the highlight of college for me."

"Bro, you sound sad as shit right now. What happened on the plantation that got you feeling solemn?" I was alarmed. This was out of character for him. "Let me ask you this, because I see the wheel turning, what side of the quarter is he on?"

Big Brains smiled.

"You have to be the most racial brother on the planet," he laughed.

"I'll stop being racial when American't starts loving Black people," I told him. "Now you know that I have never in my life said that 'all white people are racist' right?"

Big Brains crossed his arms across his chest and stood to his feet. He nodded in agreement with me.

I continued, "And the reason being is this, five hundred thousand white boys died to free us from slavery, but also, five hundred thousand white boys died to keep us enslaved. So, when I meet one of these pink crackers, I have to ask myself, 'what side of the quarter is he or she on?' The side that wants to see me free or the side that wants to ensure the perpetuity of my enslavement."

We both started laughing this time.

I stood up and pounded my chest with my right fist.

"So, before you give me the synopsis of what took place today with you and a pink cracker, what side of the quarter is he on?"

Big Brains smiled, but was silent. He didn't look at me. I could see that he was having a mental conflict, so I gave him time to gather his thoughts.

After a pause, he began illustrating the event that pushed him into the quicksand that was slowly swallowing him.

"Before today," Big Brains said. "I would have told you that the Haute brothers had my back." He pointed to me and with a wide smile he stated, "On the right side of the quarter."

He imitated my gesture, but tapped his chest lightly with both hands. His head held high he yelled, "OUR SIDE OF THE QUARTER!"

Now I was laughing at him for mocking me.

"But now I don't know. So, one of the Hautes called me to his office today, and it went down like this:"

"Glad to see you Bubba!"

"My name is Baba Maizi Ukuu."

He paused his story to remind me, "You know I hate it when people mispronounce my name; especially white people!"

"No Sir!" I interjected and raised a finger in the air. "If he is on the wrong side of the quarter, please refer to him as a pink cracker."

Big Brains threw a hand at me, and continued his story, "So the guy says, *Well don't you have a nickname for your friends?*"

"No I don't. Please call me Baba, pronounced Bay-Bay; it is my name."

"No problem, friend. Have a seat please. Do you drink or smoke? I have the best of the best if you'd like to try anything."

He motioned towards the bar but I declined.

"I was in the middle of something very important. Can you please tell me what this is about?"

"I was even more uncomfortable at this point."

"Well, the fact of the matter is this. I come from a long line of inventors. My father. My uncle. My grandfather. Hell I even have two aunts and a niece with patents. All together over the course of about 150 years, the Haute family has accumulated exactly 881 patents. And that is something that we are extremely proud of."

"Something in my stomach became extremely tight. I tried to keep a straight face."

"You should be. Even one patent should make someone proud. We Inventors contribute to society with machinations that raise the quality of life for all."

"Look here friend. You! All by yourself have accomplished 880 patents. Which is extremely." Mr. Haute started coughing then gathered himself. *"I really like how articulate you are."*

"What are you talking about?"

I didn't want to screw face and scare the pink cracker, but I knew even smiling and me being Black scares some of them. I averted

84

my eyes for a few seconds. Then I began laughing and rubbing my hands together to give me time to regain my composure.

"With all due respect Mr. Haute."

"Yes friend."

"My name is Baba. It's a very simple name to pronounce. B-A-B-A. Whatever the reason you asked to see me, can we please discuss it so that I can return to work. I know that I'm articulate because I have articulate parents."

"I digressed and inhaled as much of the air in the room that I could and held it."

He stood up and said, *"I have a confession. I'm confused as to how one man can create 880 patents in 21 years when it took my entire family 150 years to accomplish 881. It boggles my mind. It awakens me in a state of confusion. A man... who is an anomaly to even his own race."*

"I don't mean to interrupt you but George Washington Carver has over one thousand patents and he's Black as well. He's my...."

"George who? The Haute family has always had more patents than anyone else in this country. That is a FACT going back 150 years! I'm pushing the pause button on your funding," the company is receiving a lot of requests for consulting. With your skill set and capabilities of technical articulation to the most elementary mindset, you're the perfect person to represent and consult for the company. To put it frankly, friend, I just can't stomach the idea of one man showboating the Haute family legacy. Besides, this will allow you to go on an idea-hunting mission, and send those ideas back to corporate headquarters, of course."

"I already have ideas. I have books of...."

"Well, we already own those books. We'll even get you some new ones to write in during your travels; property of Haute, of course. The pause button has been pushed. The consulting opportunity is going to take you away from the laboratory and give you a chance to spend time travelling. We have partners all over the world but most of your time will need to be spent between Germany and several Asian countries."

"I didn't know that I was showboating. Your company recruited me. You told me..."

"That was a long time ago, and WOAH! WOAH! WOAH! There is no need to be aggressive!"

"He called you aggressive?" I interjected again at this point and held my hand up to Brains. I closed my eyes and shook my head. "I bet his pink ass turned red, didn't he?"

Baba continued as if he didn't even hear me, *"I was simply replying to your statement, but since I'm being aggressive, I'll aggressively see myself out."*

"Bro, that's it?" I asked. "Is this a bad thing? Travelling around the world. Can you take your family with you?"

Big Brains sat forward on the bench across from me, with his head down.

"I don't know what to do now. I went back to my lab but I couldn't work. And for what? I'm not going to get the chance to finish anything. And before you say just quit, who else is going to give me this type of creative freedom? Last year alone, my research expenditures were over one hundred million dollars. Haute and Haute spent the money without even blinking. So, I've been lounging around all day. Which is why I'm still here as a matter-of-fact. This laboratory is my baby."

"Well you won't know if you don't look. I'll have my assistant start researching your competition..." I was brainstorming until Brains cut me off.

"I signed a non-compete clause that says that if I ever quit, I cannot go to a competitor, and I cannot open a competing business anywhere in American't for at least thirty years; the time duration of a patent." Brains stated with finality.

"You were very young when you signed that contract forfeiting your intellectual property. Have you ever had Nice Head or another attorney review it since you've signed?"

Brains simply closed his eyes and shook his head.

Weighing the situation, I gave a loud exhale then stated, "Damned if you're Black and damned if you're Black. Bro, you need to wake up white, it would solve all of your problems."

For the first time that day, Baba had a gut-wrenching laugh so hard he cried. Then he just sobbed.

All those speeches by his parents to work harder and be smarter to truly be competitive were fruitless. A slave working hard will always be a slave working hard. There are no distinctions amongst slaves on plantations. Black intellectualism is a tricky possession. Some highly intelligent Black people play dumb so as not to appear to be smarter than the non-melanated that they have to work with. I could never do that. I could never agree with that tactic. Big Brains' situation was the perfect example. Although he didn't play dumb, the existence of highly intellectual Blacks is an oxymoron to some, white minds.

Seeing my friend hurt, made me hurt. I gave him some time, and tried to keep myself from getting angry at anyone hurting him. I walked around the picnic bench where I was sitting. When I thought that I heard his last sniffle, I spoke.

"You are never one to question the actions of someone white being racist. You always give people, of all colors, the benefit of doubt. What is this Baba? Is it a promotion, moving you to consulting? Is it a demotion? Because if you signed away your intellectual property, didn't they have the right to do this to you whenever they wanted? I'm asking you?"

He shook his head, but he never wiped his tears away. He allowed them to remain painted against his black canvas. A stream of disappointment tinged with confusion.

"I can honestly say that this feels like racism. Mr. Haute talked about protecting his family legacy by WHAT!"

He shot forward with his arms wide.

"By stopping me from issuing more patents than the totality of his family for the last 150 years."

He leaned back against the table and took a deep breath.

"You are always talking about different white people, classifying this white and that white, but you never talk about going to war. It's like an invisible line that you stay behind. In all these years, not once have you ever mentioned violence against these PINK CRACKERS!"

He looked at me with eyes I had never seen before. Something sinister was brewing. I was shocked that this was Big Brains speaking, but I also knew that my brother was hurt.

"Not a war Baba. Not a war brother."

I walked closer to him. Clapping my hands several times while taking a deep breath, I exhaled and began my soliloquy.

"A civil war will never work because the wrong white people would be killed. There are white people, the pink crackers, and then there are the euro tokens. The white people are our allies. They were the ones holding the 'Black Lives Matter' signs and wearing the BLM t-shirts. They stood next to us during the protest and, in some cities, they even protested for us in our absence. I define the pink crackers as those that don't acknowledge their forefathers as immigrants but they hate immigrants. The pink crackers lie and claim their race built American't through sweat and hard work, and yet they refuse to acknowledge the contribution of slavery to their very existence. They are the pale skinned purveyors of capitalism but they only think that 'they' should receive its benefits and sit at the peak of the monetary ladder. They're quick to claim that they don't see race and everything is an economics game. ZERO SUM! But you have to see through the illusion. Most pink crackers are poor like 'US,' and yet they forever drudge to the whims of the euro tokens."

"Now peep game, there actually is an economics war. But what the pink crackers don't realize is that they are being used by the euro tokens to protect the euro tokens' banks, land, homes, and other corporate properties. It is the euro tokens that own the white, media propaganda machine, and actually sit at the top 1% of the economic totem pole. It is the euro tokens against everyone else, which is why it DOES NOT make any sense that pink crackers could ever be Republican. But it is through the white, media propaganda machine that euro tokens make pink crackers believe that they are on the same side, and convinced them to vote against their best interest."

"Rich, euro tokens only care about other rich, euro tokens. So, if we started a race war, the rich, euro tokens will simply flee to their private planes and yachts and bounce to Europe or their villas in the Maldives. While the economically poor Blacks will be killing the economically poor, pink crackers. And if that happens, WE ALL LOSE! Because once the smoke settles, those euro tokens will return to American't and find new bodies to replace the poor ones that were killed, Black, white and pink. THERE CAN NEVER BE A RACE WAR! UNLESS, like I mentioned earlier, we let these white folks and pink crackers go at it, while we sit on the sideline and barbecue. The euro tokens control the plantation and they know it's about economics, but as long as these pink crackers make it a priority to believe they're more equal to the rich than their equally poor Black and brown neighbors, they will continue to fall for the distraction of racial fuckery. DuBois explains this very clearly. This man looked one hundred years into the future and every word he has spoken and written about this country still applies."

I pumped a fist in the air, hyped from my own deduction of the races.

"Now think about this Brains, how in the hell Mr. Haute never heard of George Washington Carver. Not only the greatest inventor of the Black race, still to this day, but the greatest inventor of the world PERIOD! But if you look up patents from his inventions, whose names are on them? The pink crackers that owned him. And to make matters worse, the white media propaganda machine wants us to believe that his owners castrated him because they had daughters, but that's bullshit. They castrated George Washington Carver to ensure he didn't leave a legacy behind that could question the ownership of his inventions, and demand to get paid. They castrated him to ensure that the pink cracker family that owned him, their own future family members would get paid in perpetuity. And if we really were to go back and analyze the Haute family one hundred and fifty years ago, I guarantee that at least half of that eight hundred and eighty one inventions that he is bragging about, came from the genius of the slaves that the family owned. They made their money the same way every other rich, euro token made their money, from the slavery of Black people."

Big Brains was watching me, but his right hand seemed to be playing the piano when he chimed, "DAMN Bro! Another George."

Brains shook his head after realizing the similarity of first names between George Washington Carver and George Floyd, both castrated by a pink cracker.

"So I have to keep watching more Georges die because the pink crackers keep falling for the booby trap? So what's going to happen once they run out of Georges? They move to the next letter in the alphabet?"

The imaginary piano stopped at the thought and question.

Baba hit me with a question that made me think.

"Bro, we can solve racism overnight!" It wasn't the best answer but it was all that I could think of. I shrugged my shoulders and let the question slide off somewhere onto the floor.

"I'm listening." Big Brains stated in the way that always made me feel like he already knew what I was going to say.

"If white people cleaned their closet, all the racist, pink crackers would be dead tomorrow, and the euro tokens would lose their value. The pink crackers have relatives and a lot of those relatives like Jay-Z and Beyonce, and were at the Nas concerts. I went to a Nas concert and only saw one other Black man the entire night. When Nas screamed *'where my niggas at'* every white person in the building responded as loud as they could *'I'M RIGHT HERE!'* I was literally discombobulated because, technically, only the janitor and I should have responded."

"So, what is the possibility of the euro tokens cashing chips?" Big Brains asked. "Right now everybody is talking about reparations, right? This might actually be a time in history where the powerful share the wealth in a manner that's permanent for the Black race."

"Not being mean brother because you know that I love you, but are the Haute brothers sharing with you? Are the Haute brothers asking you for your input on some reparations they got planned?"

I shrugged my shoulders and shook my head.

"I will say it today, tomorrow, next week and next year," I continued. "I think we should let the conscientious white brothers and sisters that we have on our side, that's on the right side and the Black side, go to war with their pink cracker relatives. They are related. I MEAN DAMN, what do you think the CIVIL WAR WAS? It was white family members against white family members. We sit on the side and barbecue until it's over!"

We both laughed.

"The civil war in this country was between good, white boy versus evil, confederate, pink cracker. So, let the second civil war be the same thing. We'll make the announcement on BET, because the white brothers that love us will get the announcement that if their white asses wore a 'Black Lives Matter' t-shirt, they are obligated to kill their pink cracker and racist family members that they know exist, and have been putting up with every year at the Thanksgiving dinner. They're always telling nigger jokes but since our white brothers and sisters don't laugh, it's been okay for them not to say anything or make any moral demands. I call BULLSHIT! White people need to clean THEIR FUCKING CLOSETS!"

Baba was smiling again. He stood up and opened his arms wide to welcome me into a hug. I embraced my brother and squeezed him as tight as I could.

He patted me on the back and said, "You always have a way with words Bro."

Releasing our embrace, I looked him in the eyes.

"But do you feel better?"

He walked toward the exit door of the courtyard and I followed alongside him.

"We both know at the end of the day, I'm going to do whatever my wife tells me. It is her and my family that is more important than a job. If she tells me to stay, I'll stay. And if she tells me that she wants to travel, we'll travel."

I nodded my head in agreement. I sensed my rational brother was back in his sane state of mind.

I returned the compliment.

"Smart man brother, you have always been a very smart man."

12

....

THINKING ABOUT JaJa, Silent Saint and Big Brains, I came to the realization that Black people slither. You can't walk on or in white shit, you must maneuver through it. We perform mental acrobatics and physical contortions like circus aberrations caged for the white folk to point at or stare as if we are anything but actually humans. I apologize to Ota Benga. I apologize to you Sara Baartman. Their treatment was a precursor to future legislation deeming *'waking up Black a crime.'*

We don't walk with chest out and shoulders back as if this is our country. The melanated culture walks differently. Black people slithẽr. Heads down trying not to be noticed, trying not to attract or gain attention. So we simply try to ignore everything, even ourselves and especially our own history. Too many Black firsts had to come back because someone at the corporate office reminded them that the color they woke up wearing was inappropriate for the boardroom. You got promoted, now what? You got elected, now what? You still need our permission. You still need our approval.

Even the first Black President didn't receive the respect that he deserved while occupying the White House. Damn his Black, uppity ass for thinking he could evade the laws of American't; so they had to remind him, even *HIM*! So he slithered and forgot about us.

I apologize to President Barack Hussein Obama for you and your family enduring over twenty-seven hundred death threats per day for eight years. Maybe he forgot about the rest of us because he was trying to survive like the rest of us; there was a warrant for his arrest because he kept waking up Black!

Black people slither, heads down wetting the ground and floors with our tears. We keep waiting for acknowledgement. We keep waiting for a new flag, a new national anthem, and a new constitution that includes us. We keep waiting for the white folk to give us permission to hold our heads up and walk, and call us American; minus the 'hyphen' or 'minus sign' depending on your interpretation.

I was lying in bed delivering a mental tirade to nobody willing to listen. I was still pissed at JaJa and the category of Black he represented. At FAMU the brothers and I would huddle, each placing a hand in the middle of the circle and yelling the FAMU motto, 'BLACK ON BLACK EVERYTHING' always ending in laughter. And to think the entire time JaJa was placing his hand in the middle but not his heart.

Earlier that day when I was on the phone, Lava had walked into my office.

Classy, always confident, she closed the door behind her and walked to the window.

I watched her every move; of her hands, her eyes, the movement of her legs. I watched the way she turned her head to look at me or away from me. It was our dance routine. She kept her on shoes if she didn't want to have sex and took them off when she did.

When I hung up the phone, she turned around.

"How is your day going so far?" She asked, keeping on her shoes.

"Well that depends on you," I smiled. "You have an amazing way of building up a certain anticipation in me. Call me a Pavlovian hound. I'm just waiting on the bell to ring."

"Tell me, why do you read so much Black history?"

"I sit on the board of directors for two nonprofits. When Sandra Bland was killed, I was there immediately to protest. Eric Garner, Mike Brown, name all or any of the unarmed, innocent Black men

94

or women who were killed by a white policeman and I was there on the front lines protesting. Studying the history of American't helps me put everything into context."

Lava interrupted me, "Like working here on the plantation?"

"That part! But I wouldn't see the plantation if I were ignorant. An ignorant Black man would just be happy to possess a job. Not realizing the context of where he's standing. Black bodies built Wall Street but black hands didn't get any stock options for doing so."

"But there has to be more than just understanding context. What are you going to do with all of the information that you're accumulating? Write a book? Give a speech? Run for Governor of North Carolina?"

She stood with her arms crossed and laying on her chest.

"Do you have a chip on your shoulder?" She asked sarcastically. "Did something happen that I don't know about? Would you even care to share with me?"

Before I could respond, she yelled, "POWER TO THE PEOPLE BLACK MAN!" With her raised right fist in the air, eyes closed and head back. She dropped her hand and started laughing.

"You remind me so much of my husband that I have these moments where I feel like God is playing a trick on me. You both say the same things but you are really doing nothing to only amount to nothing. He never wrote a book. He never gave a speech. And he definitely strayed from politics."

"Excuse me but I believe the trick is on me. You have a helluva way of building me up and empowering me and my masculinity, only to tear it down with what seems to be your favorite phrase. Which is that '*I remind you of your fucking husband!*' Enough of that shit already. You don't have to say that no more."

If I could scare her I would, but I'm sure it would backfire. I remained seated. Even my ego is not that stupid.

Bringing a hand to her chest, she became wide-eyed with mouth agape.

"Well excuse me! Are you on your period? Did I kick you in the vagina or are you using your balls this morning?"

She walked back and forth shaking her head.

"My husband was always coming home complaining about the white man. The white man did this, RACIST! The white man did that, DISCRIMINATION! The white man, the white man, the Goddamn white man. Just like him, you get quiet as hell on payday. Oh yeah, this Friday is payday. There ain't no discussion about the plantation on payday. Goodbye Mary Mcleod Bethune. Goodbye Medger Evers. Goodbye Harriet Tubman. Can't talk today because the white man don' put money in my account."

She clapped her hands and started laughing harder this time. A very hard laugh, as if she had been holding it and could finally let go. Or maybe she was laughing at me and her husband.

"Oh my god!" She yelled. "My husband got promoted and found himself in the room with the big boys drinking scotch and smoking a cigar, when one of the founders of his firm looked at him and said, 'you're not like the other ones so you'll appreciate this joke.'"

She turned to look me in the eyes.

"It was a nigger joke. He told me there was this moment inside of him where, the fire inside, burned louder than it ever did as these white men surrounding him were all laughing. And just like that, he realized that he was laughing too. That fire inside died with that laugh. That was the moment my husband became neutered. Spayed like a mutt off the street. It was a test and he failed. He knew he failed. So I'm looking at you and I'm asking you, how are you going to find balance? The higher you get promoted the whiter it gets. Are you going to keep those balls you're proudly displaying this morning, or will you get castrated for the money? I mean it's bad enough that you fuck white women, but you're so quick to scream about Black history?" She threw a hand in my direction and loudly sucked her teeth.

I stood up and walked from behind my desk and put my hands in my pockets. I leaned against the desk.

"First of all," I said. "No one is buying me. I'll be damned if a cracker is dumb enough to make an attempt to even think about a nigger joke in my presence. And secondly, when I fuck white women, they all get HATE DICK!"

I smiled waiting for her to acknowledge the statement. Once her head snapped in my direction, I continued.

"And it's HATE DICK because their great grand-daddy stole my great grand-daddy's land."

I started laughing but she never joined me. She was standing but moving around in her own mind. I wished that I knew what she was thinking about. She is so damn intelligent and beautiful.

I walked over to where she stood and spoke as I looked out the window. I held a vivid picture in my head, like a video of myself sitting in the picture that was being painted all around me. I stuttered, finding it difficult to speak.

"I- I have these mo'.... moments with you where I really don't know if you love me for reminding you of your husband, or do you hate me for the memories between you and him that I resurrect? Are you attacking me? Or are you attacking him right now? Because your husband is not standing in front of you. So whatever's going on between you two, please take it out on that Negro when you get home. I don't want to start my morning arguing with a woman that's not even mine."

She turned to face me, almost allowing her nose to touch my lips.

"Have you ever had sex with a neutered, Black man?" She asked me. "Of course you haven't. I'm frustrated and tired of fighting. I'm tired of listening to Black men cry, whine, and pout about the damn white man, the system, or the corporate plantation. I'm in my fifties. I think I see the end and I really just want to fuck. And I want to fuck someone other than my husband. I chose to fuck you and ended up listening to someone that sounds just like my husband."

I was still trying to figure out where the anger came from.

"Hence the frustration with your marriage?"

"Ooooohhhh pookie-pooh! That is so sweet that you are actually trying to get inside of my head and heart. Now let me help you with whatever is going on inside of yours. There is NO love and there is NO relationship. It is a situationship where we fuck each other for convenience."

She cleared her throat for dramatic effect, then crossed her arms across her chest.

"The gay guy file, Mr. Keon Patience. Did you note everything that you were supposed to? That was a special case, hence the reason it was given to you. You're a man that makes very few mistakes and we didn't need any made with that specific termination."

I laughed.

"Did you just reverse ninja my shit?"

I realized what she did and I tried to act like it didn't hurt. I wanted to tell her that I actually loved her, but she reached into the clouds and pulled out the Gay Guy. I did my best to match her coldness with coldness, but something broke inside of me.

"I've noted every damn thing that I'm supposed to by regulation. And I knew the regulations like the back of my hands. I didn't miss anything. Now were we talking about you and I, or you and your husband?"

"Answer my FUCKING QUESTION!" Lava demanded. Asking but not waiting for an actual reply. "I have a meeting with Mr. Lamour this afternoon about that file."

She waved a finger in my face.

"That's not good for you. I don't sit in front of that man unless something is wrong. So, I'm giving you an opportunity to tell me right now. Is there anything that you can think of at this moment, that just maybe, you forgot to put in his file? Or stood out that you decided not to note that could have been of importance? So important that it's coming back to bite you in the ass."

"If I forgot when I did it, then I'm still forgetting. I do everything by regulation no matter what. Male or female. Black, white, Hispanic, Asian or one of those Tiger Woods' babies. What is he 'splasian?'"

"If you fucked up anything, I will be the one to fire your ass. We don't have a relationship, okay! I simply fuck you IF I'm in the mood or tired of what's lying beside me at home. Don't get it TWISTED you fake ass DuBois! You're either dreaming or delusional."

She walked out in the most theatrical fashion, leaving the door open. Then the queen returned.

"And by the way, I don't have to *'reverse ninja'* because I'm a FUCKING NINJA and that's why you didn't see this coming!"

I was fuming to a point, I'm pretty sure steam was coming off my head and shoulders. I had to hit something, but I had the restraint to never hit a woman. I waited just long enough to make sure that she was no longer on my office floor. I stormed out straight for the gym, to my locker.

I was hitting the punching bag with everything I had. Punch, punch, kick, knee. Punch, punch, kick, knee. Elbow, knee, elbow, knee. I threw punches with everything I had in me. Trying not to hear her voice. Her sarcasm. Her control. I tried to throw everything I had into that punching bag until I passed out. And just when I thought that I would, a towel landed on my face. I stopped, breathing hard, held my head down so that the towel could fall off. When I looked up it was Mr. Jahiem Jury standing there looking at me with concern.

The elder spoke, "Whatever's bothering you, son, let's go talk about it."

He nodded his head as if I'd already agreed.

At first I didn't want to, but then I realized I needed to get things off my chest. I simply shook my head to affirm that I'd talk with him, and walked to the locker room.

Afterward, we went to a nearby bar.

Sitting down with an elder that I held in high regard was the medication that I needed. It was simply therapeutic. I started talking and couldn't stop. Everything that was being held flooded out onto the bar and into the ear of Mr. Jury.

He said absolutely nothing, never interrupting me or giving me a shocked look or even a look of disappointment. He merely raised a finger to get the bartender's attention, slid his glass to the side, waited for another drink and held his head forward at the bar. Not even glancing in my direction.

Then I finished. More exhausted spewing my confusion about my father's decision to choose homelessness, sleeping with my married neighbor, and being pimped smacked by my boss.

I also felt stupid after hearing myself speak so candidly about my life. I thought I was smart.

I waited for Mr. Jury to determine that deduction.

He took his time, like old, Black men do. Every now and then he made a grunt. He slid his glass back and forth between his hands. I waited like a schoolboy in timeout, waiting for the teacher to free me. He finally turned in my direction and began speaking.

"I'm seventy years old and I've pretty much seen and heard it all. Nothing that you're doing is an invention and women have always made men do strange things."

He pointed to himself.

"And I've done much worse than fuck a neighbor or office sex." He smiled. "The only thing that I can tell you about women is that they are dangerous. And there is nothing more dangerous than 'P-power' with a title bigger than yours. That girl is definitely going to fire you so you might as well get prepared. Get it in your head NOW! She's going to fire you for the same reason that she likes to see you naked; you remind her of her husband. You really need to think about that. She's abusing you because she's powerless at home. But, what's done is done. Your neighbor, well... he sucked his teeth, I've had a few of those too. At least you're smart enough not to go into her house. That doesn't exactly make it better but be careful with that one too. Maybe you'll get lucky and she'll leave her husband and move away."

He got a good laugh from that one. He seemed to share a memory with himself, something from the past came and went.

"Now for Mr. Lamour, my buddy. I think it's funny that there are so many amazing and highly educated Blacks in corporate America. But even with all that education we are still just a bunch of niggas walking around a cereal bowl throwing fruit loops at each other." He shakes his head disapprovingly. "Lamour founded the plantation you work on. Did you ever think about what he had to go through to get to where he is today? He worked on one corporate plantation and then rose to own his own plantation."

I wanted to interrupt so badly but knew that it was my turn to be quiet and listen.

"He provides jobs for thousands of Black folk across this nation. For a history buff, did you ever think about 'his' story? The man is two years older than me. We grew up at a time when Black people had to get off the sidewalk if someone white was walking toward us. We had to hold our head down and not look a white person in the eyes."

"You ever wonder how many times that man had to swallow his pride? Keep quiet surrounded by the white boys and all the nigga jokes. Telling yourself over and over to stay focused because you had billionaire goals and billionaire dreams. He's a fucking billionaire. At a time when the average Black person thought that if you possessed ten thousand dollars you were rich. Here comes a Black man with a destiny to generate a billion dollars. He's a goddamn genius by any measure. Of course you don't like him, you're not supposed to. You are supposed to respect him. Anything he does, or says, is out of a strong reverence to toughen you up. Prepare you for the white man's un-United States."

He took a sip of his drink and continued.

"He was and is smart enough to keep that *'white voice'* in your head for when you leave his plantation and go work somewhere else. And that white voice is in all of our heads, educated Negroes get a triple, double dose because we allow ourselves to be exposed even longer to the white public education propaganda machine. It's that *implanted* white voice that reminds you that you are a NIGGA. You're the one that ran and got all those degrees and started thinking that you're not like the other Blacks. Lamour knows that if he takes away that white voice, you'll fuck around thinking your equal to these white boys and get yourself killed. He says exactly what he knows the white folk would say to keep all your Black asses in check."

Mr. Jury continued, "When the civil rights started, I say this, no we didn't march and hold signs, but Lamour was the first one in line to write a check. He always had to stay in the shadows to not agitate the white boys holding a microscope over him; constantly waiting for the opportunity to attack him. Just waiting for him to be too Black to be a member. Too Black to be invited. But whether it was Elderidge Cleaver, Fannie Lou Hamer, or Shirley Chisholm, he was in the background providing financial support. So any hang ups that you have against that giant is misdirected and frankly, I would even go so far as to say that you owe him an apology. You're one of the few to have the privilege of his mentorship."

He finally sat staring at me with his arms wide open.

"But why a plantation?" I asked.

Mr. Jury looked at me quizzically.

I continued, "Why rise so high, provide so many jobs for your own people and foster the same atmosphere as your white counterparts that ultimately abuse you? That's the part that I can't figure out."

"Because his plantation is a very small one on a much larger plantation and he has to play by the same damn rules. You want his plantation to be singular or isolated? You're not thinking. Even with all his money, his plantation is still located in the un-United States. This is whiteboy country, their own personal playground. And true he's a billionaire, but the number one rule of the rich, staying rich, is never use your own money. So he still has to jump through hoops to appease the white folk if he wants to be a part of their economics. Because economics is something, no Black person has. Oh yeah, a Black man can make money in this country, but a Black man cannot *generate* economics in this country. The gatekeeper is always going to be white in this un-United plantation called America. Mr. Lamour is a giant. Give him the respect that he deserves."

Mr. Jury rose out of his bar stool and grasped me with both hands at arms distance.

"One more thing young lad. Don't ever connect your soul to your job. It's a job and nothing else. It is not why you were created. You're not a job title, you are a man. And a job is a job. Your true work is in the heart."

He relinquished his grasp and poked me in the heart with a finger and a smile.

There were several women throughout the bar area. As I embraced Mr. Lamour and offered my goodbyes, a very beautiful, white woman approached me with a bag of skittles with her name on one side and her phone number on the other. She gently kissed me on the cheek and then turned around to walk back to her table. I watched her the entire time, and so did Mr. Jury.

I was still locked in on the table when Mr. Jury said, "What the fuck she give you a bag of skittles for? You young'uns are always doing things that just don't make much sense anymore; well, at least not to me." He shook his head and threw a hand in the air.

"Today, you were the teacher." I placed the skittles in the inner pocket of my sports coat. "Next time we talk, I'mma teach you about these." I patted my pocket and laughed.

"Well I can't eat candy," the elder said. "I'm wearing dentures now. So, I don't need to know about any candy, Skittles or Snickers."

As I walked him out, I patted him on the back, "Well I think you're going to like this candy!"

Mr. Jury turned serious.

"You know what I'm about to ask you son?" He was wide-eyed with anticipation of my answer.

I dropped my head. "No, I have not joined a church, and no, I'm not getting married any time soon."

"You are always asking me why I got married, and I have something recent that happened to me that I want to share. Now if you have to be somewhere let me know, but I can give you the short version." He put his jacket on as he waited for me to respond.

I know damn well that old, Black men do not possess any type of short version.

"No rush," I said. "But the short version would help."

"Understood. Well, I got sick recently. I was lying in bed feeling absolutely horrible. Sweating, coughing, nauseated and ten other ailments. I took all the medication that I was supposed to. Beebae was nursing me like she always does during these times. But this one particular time, I was in and out of consciousness and when I came to, she had placed my head in her lap, rubbed my head, and she sang to me. Usually, with a migraine, the slightest touch or the slightest sound, feels or sounds a thousand times harder or louder and drove me insane. But in that moment, I felt a sense of serenity enter my body from the tip of her fingers into my cranium down to the tips of my big toes."

He poked a finger into my chest.

"It was love that healed me son. Now you tell me which one of these one-night, lollipop girls would take the time to nurse you when you're down, number one, or take the time to hold you and pour love into your soul to heal you? Fun girls are just that, fun girls. Lollipops are good until they're gone. You can suck that lollipop as slow as you'd like, but the end is still the same. You'll be holding a piece of plastic and a fun memory. You're a good guy and you need a good woman. But you can't find what you ain't looking for, and you won't appreciate what's in front of you if you just want to lick on someone for temporary fun."

He turned towards the exit and grunted.

"Always parting with words of wisdom," I said while walking by his side.

"I guess the young ladies don' went from lollipops to skittles."

He winked at me.

"Oh, back in the day, I licked all kinds of lollipops. Have your fun son, but there's more to a woman than just her skittles. Please do me the honor of remembering that."

He tilted his hat at me and then made his exit.

13

SILENT SAINT STARED in the mirror. Wisdom Saintinus wanted to be sure every hair on his head was in place, he became ashamed of himself for being angry about cutting his hair. Such a superficial sacrifice compared to his savior dying on the cross for our sins.

He was tested and failed. The vanity derived from his dread-locks angered the Lord, and it was the Lord that punished him. He prayed silently, this cleaner look demanded by the white Bishop had nothing to do with his Blackness. How could he have allowed himself to be so easily fooled by the devil? He rose from his knees to answer the request for prayer by a member of the congregation.

After graduating from FAMU he attended divinity school at Emory University. Upon receipt of his Divinity Doctorate, he became an Assistant Pastor at the Mecklenburg Methodist Episcopal Church, the largest multi-racial church in the state of North Carolina. After twenty years he was now serving as the Supervisory Pastor of the Humanitarian Chapter of the church. He could easily send a junior Pastor but he meticulously selected certain members whom he assisted with prayer himself, and this was one of those special considerations. As he exited the mirror, he turned to grab his bible and leave.

"Thank God you haven't left yet. I was worried I'd have to call you with instructions to turn around."

The white Bishop smiled as he walked over to place a hand on Mr. Saintinus' left shoulder.

Bishop Raeford Whimper did not see color. But if he did, it would be the color green. Churches needed money; especially if they planned on obtaining longevity. He was shorter than Silent Saint, the top of the Bishop's head stopped right at his shoulder. He was also extremely pale. His skin saw very little sun. He was a natural redhead, and at age seventy-five, he still possessed a mane of flaming red hair. He adjusted his glasses to allow his brownish-green eyes to pierce into the soul of Silent Saint.

"Is there a problem Bishop?" He returned the smile with a look of concern.

"The Polk family has been the largest tither to our church for decades. Mrs. Polk called me specifically to ask that I send someone else and not you. And when a Polk asks us for a favor, we make sure that we respond accordingly, so ease your mind and allow me to supervise the arrangements for this one."

He patted the obedient servant on the shoulder and turned to exit the room.

"But is there a problem? I don't understand. In twenty years you have never intervened at my request to assist anyone. I know every member of the family and feel a certain honor in offering my prayers to them in their time of need. And why would it matter to you who went? I have eight pastors serving under me but because it is the Polk family, I didn't want to take this lightly. Regardless of financial contribution, it is incumbent for us...."

The Bishop did not want to have to repeat Mrs. Polk's specific demands, but he could only be so patient.

"I can't lie to you, and I don't want to make you upset. However, it's not so much as not wanting you specifically, the request was more so that I send someone of their same race."

He watched his friend step back and grab the cross hanging on his necklace.

"You don't have any administrative experience, so let me tell you this, contributions ALWAYS MATTER! They are the lifeblood of the church."

"Forgive me for interjecting Bishop. I say with all due respect Sir, this is a church and the lifeblood is and always will be the praying souls that show up in this building to honor our savior. It is their souls and the blood of Jesus...."

Wisdom was speaking quicker than he wanted and he began to hear his heartbeat over his own voice.

"And I hate to interrupt you AGAIN but I'm the last person that you ever have to quote a scripture to. We are a church, and we are a business."

The Bishop began walking away from his friend and closer to the only stained window in the room. "Do you know how much this one window cost?" He pointed at the window. "Have you ever seen the church's light bill? Water bill? Do you know how much it costs to replace the roof of a building this size?"

The men locked eyes.

Wisdom closed his eyes and placed his chin in his chest. He was consciously praying as he stood in silence.

"You are allowing a racist act by complying with this request. Our Christian doctrine dictates..."

"It dictates that we not be foolish and bite the hand that FEEDS US! I don't know the cost of the window or the roof replacement, but I do know that the Polk family paid for every stained window in the church and when we needed a roof, they wrote the check."

"Now I'm telling you as your senior leader that you are not to go to the Polk's home for any reason whatsoever. It is one request, racist or not, that we will comply for the purpose of keeping this family happy. And if I have to choose between making them happy or confusing *you*, then I suggest that you take your confusion, open your bible and start praying for clarity. You're a good man and this is a tough decision, but it's also decisions like these that have stumped your progress here for promotions."

"There's God's way and there's man's way. Man is not as perfect as God. We are not here to issue judgment and we are not here to fight for racial equality. We are here to ensure, by any means necessary, the continuity of this church by proselytizing the foundation of Christianity. This conversation is over and I expect to see you in an hour to host the Inner Circle of Prayer meeting. I'm told that we have some special guests and I want you to oversee the program."

"You choose money." Wisdom said it in a whisper. He felt a sharp pain in his chest and light headed.

"What?" The Bishop turned at the door to face him, exasperated.

Wisdom was beyond himself and thundered "HAVE YOU CHOSEN MONEY?" The yell emptied his lungs and reverberated off of the expensive, stained window.

The white Bishop opened the door to exit, and without looking at his injured brother in Christ, he said, "If you have to ask that question, then you don't know what a church is."

Pastor Wisdom Saintinus was vehement with anger as he stood in his private office bathroom splashing water onto his face.

This didn't happen. They were the largest, multi-racial church in Charlotte! They were the largest, multi-racial church in North Carolina. Their members just didn't see color. They were taught, and preached, to only see their fellow Christian brothers and sisters as imperfect children in the eyes of Christ. Was Christ simply testing him again? Was he not supposed to cut his hair?

He stormed out of the bathroom, grabbed his briefcase and bolted to his vehicle. The children of the Lord may be imperfect, but that didn't mean that he had to put up with every imperfection.

He started the car and pounced the steering wheel. *This didn't happen.* Why was he so furious? He felt something he had never experienced before. He was told that his color prevented him from doing what he loved most. This is what God had prepared him to do, trained him to do, blessed him to do, and now his color was denying him the ability to perform God's work.

He spoke to the empty car, "There's God's law and there's man's foolishness. If the Lord is with me, then who shall stand against me."

He drove to the address of the Polk family. The Bishop did not speak for his Savior!

He prayed and repeated scripture all the way to the large home.

While sitting in the driveway, he was convinced that when his fellow Christians would see him, they would find fault in their request, repent and ask him and the Lord for forgiveness.

All of this was some form of miscommunication. The Bishop had to have misinterpreted the message that he received. Wisdom rang the doorbell.

The younger Mrs. Polk answered the door. She was the daughter of the older Mrs. Polk who laid in bed needing prayer. She walked out onto the porch and closed the door behind her. She brought her hands together as if praying and bowed her head with her eyes closed. She waved her hands and cleared her throat.

"I do apologize but I was hoping to prevent your arrival. I called the church back and spoke to the Bishop personally. Did you not get the message?"

"I got wayward communication that made no sense to me. I have prayed with you and your family for over twenty years as members. I've participated and prayed over special occasions at the church on multiple....."

"But that was AT-THE-CHURCH and not our home. We have never invited any of your people to our home." She stood upright as if her words gave her a new surge of strength. "Why would you think that it's okay for you to come here?"

"We are brothers and sisters of a large Christian family. It is our mutual belief in Jesus..."

"I don't mean to cut you off but I have to attend to my mother. Please send someone else of our race. My mother was born in 1934 and she has her ways. It's not personal; I'm just trying to honor my mother's dying request."

Seeing the confusion in the Pastor's face, she decided to elaborate.

"You see if she should pass the last face she sees cannot be that of a Black man."

"Can I ask you one question? Just one question please."

Mrs. Polk was standing back in her home about to close the door. She opened it a little wider without speaking.

"After your mother dies, what will be your request? I understand that racism is taught. But it doesn't have to be taught in perpetuity. You can be the one to end this. You can be the one to invite me in to show your children something different. You and I are the same age. We both were born in 1975, so let the culture and ways of 1934 die with your mother. I will pray for you. I will pray that you have the strength to choose differently when your time comes to meet our Lord and Savior. No one said being a Christian was easy, but it is us whom the devil loves most. Remove the devil from your home and allow the love of Christ to take its rightful place."

"The devil has never set foot in this house. We're just trying to make sure that niggers don't EITHER!" Mrs. Polk, breathing heavily, stared at him for several seconds and then slammed the door.

As the Pastor walked back to his car, his cell phone rang and it was the Bishop.

14

....

NICE HEAD SAT at his desk and contemplated his next move. The meeting started in seventy-five seconds. He stared at his watch, then rose to put on his suit jacket. He held the doorknob to his office took a deep breath and said *"Fuck it"* in an exasperated tone that only he could hear.

The meeting started in its usual procedural format. The closer it got to him speaking the louder his heart pounded. The thump in his chest became obnoxious footsteps racing up a staircase.

The attorney told himself "I can do this."

"Hearing no questions, does anyone have anything to share before moving to the next subject?" the President completed a quick scan of the conference table.

Attorney Hamilton Nicely stood and cleared his throat, "Good morning everyone. As the newly appointed Chief Diversity Officer for the firm, I want to place a subject on the table for discussion and vote please. I would like that vote preferably today before the close of business."

The President seemed irritated by the request, "Why the urgency?"

Being prepared for that specific question, the attorney quickly responded, "Well the city is in an uproar. Our state and our country are in an uproar. Watching the murder of George Floyd broke something in my spirit. As a matter of fact, I think it broke the spirit of every Black-American in this country. Their love of country. Their hopes. The illusion of any type of equality in this country between Black and white was shattered over the course of nine minutes and twenty-nine seconds."

"So what are you getting at? What does the protest have to do with your capacity as the Diversity Officer CHIEF?"

"What I'm getting at is this firm should utilize this opportunity to make a statement that we support Black Lives Matter. Not just for publicity but out of compassion for all of your non-white partners, employees and constituents. We can use this as an opportunity to show that we stand on the side of right. That you...uh, WE empathize with the plight of the non-white citizens of this country."

Attorney Nicely smiled while observing the reactions of those at the table; especially the President of the Company, who at the moment, appeared to be a sitting block of ice.

A junior competitor bellowed, "So why don't we run an All Lives Matter campaign instead of choosing sides there, CHIEF?"

The President held a hand.

"I don't see how this would benefit the image of our firm." He said. "All of our clients and constituents are not one color. They are a multitude of ethnicities and races. If we advertise that we stand with Black Lives Matter, what will we have to say next....?" He shrugged his shoulders. "All Hispanic Lives Matter or All Asian Lives Matter, it will never end. Hell, I'd hate to have to say ALL Indian Lives Matter, my great, great grandfather would roll over in his grave and curse me."

The President chuckled at his own humor.

Attorney Nicely maintained his cool and replied, "What is the purpose of me being the Chief Diversity Officer if nothing that I bring to the table, for the sake of diversity, gets addressed? Unarmed white people are not being shot by white cops, nor are unarmed Asians being gratuitously slaughtered by white cops; however, our Hispanic brethren often share our plight. BUT, let's say that the white cops were gratuitously killing unarmed white people. It is the history of slavery that Blacks in this country carry on their shoulders that makes the killings unequal or non-comparative to other races. ALL LIVES DON'T MATTER!"

The President interrupted, "I've heard enough. I want to pause this meeting, everyone, and ask that you leave and give me some privacy with Hamilton."

The white man was turning red around his collar.

Nice Head felt more courageous the more he spoke. 'Never back down to the white boys in the office or in the courtroom' is what his professors had instilled in their students. His favorite professor, Dr. Curry, had a sign in his class that he would make them read over and over, 'EVERY ARGUMENT IS A BATTLE, WIN!'

As everyone was vacating the room, his nemesis, Edgar spoke, "Sir with all due respect, I'd like to stay as a second voice of reason on this topic. Being that I'm not Black, I would like to ensure fairness and consideration of my race. Not saying that you are not capable but I don't see how a second opinion would hurt."

He came closer to where the white President was sitting and took a seat. He gave Hamilton a sly smile and quick wink of an eye.

The President was still sitting, right fist at his jaw and leaning in the opposite direction of where Nice Head was standing.

"Mr. Nicely you graduated from a college that I never even heard of, but we brought you on board in an effort to start giving you people an opportunity you wouldn't otherwise have. We sent you for training on diversity to help make recommendations to the firm on ways that we can ensure an image of togetherness and solidarity for all colors *at this firm*. We even voted to hang a Kwanza sign in the corporate dining facility during Christmas. But what you're asking right now is just beyond the borders of where this firm stands.

"So you're speaking for the entire firm? You are the one who told me that you would take an impartial stance on all recommendations and allow everyone at the conference table to vote. And siding with Black Lives Matter is not choosing sides, its choosing that you believe that Black people are human and deserve to be treated as such, no matter the reason. No white police officer has the right to take a man's life based on the color of his skin, and in this country, when it does happen, that color has a high probability of being Black."

Now Nice Head was losing his cool, and no longer thinking nicely.

Edgar chimed-in, "I don't know what they teach at HBCUs or if you even had books, but your next training should be at a police station. Do you know how hard it is for police in this country? If we run an ad Sir, I think we should be the firm that states Blue Lives Matter in our support for protection and civility. We should not advocate for a bunch of animals running through the street, destroying property for the sake of stealing tennis shoes, rims, bling-bling and God knows what else they pray to."

It was just too much; Hamilton's inner-Nigga broke free on the plantation.

"SHUT THE FUCK UP EDGAR! THOSE ANIMALS ARE MY PEOPLE! Sir please kick his ass out of here because he is not helping."

Hamilton closed his eyes and squeezed his hands.

"I'm really trying right now Sir, you need to get him out of here."

He opened his eyes and gave Edgar the stare of death.

The President raised a hand again and motioned for Edgar to be quiet.

"It is my understanding that after some research it was revealed that George Floyd was a repeat convict. We cannot promote the adulation of an organization that allows criminals to join or may even be a possible hate group that threatens the very fabric of our just society. In case you didn't know, I also discovered, to my dismay, that the founders of Black Lives Matter are lesbians. Did you know this?"

He didn't wait for an answer.

"I cannot be impartial to your request for a vote when you show such poor judgment in your recommendations."

Still trying to re-cage the inner-beast, Hamilton attempted to laugh.

"Nothing you're saying has anything to do with the fact that unarmed Black men are constantly being killed in the streets like dogs. That means that our society is not so just. Or maybe it is only just for white people. The man was murdered in front of the world and his previous record has nothing to do with the fact that he was not treated with the dignity of being human."

The President stood up and breathed a heavy sigh to ensure that Hamilton heard it.

"We have discussed this subject a lot longer than I intended. Come up with something else or nothing at all. Your request is denied."

He waved at Edgar.

"Get everyone back in here. Mr. Hamilton Nicely, I really think you need to consider your future at this firm." He placed both hands on the table as he continued, "I didn't select you to be the Diversity Officer to insult me with Black shit pertaining to your family members. Black is not the only color that lives outside the walls of this firm."

"It is my understanding that the definition of diversity centers around the word VA-RI-E-TY Mr. Nicely. So give me something that has variety and not just black, and you and I will be on the same page. Now, I have a meeting to run and quite frankly I don't want to see your face for the rest of the day. So fuck off and go for a walk. Not a Black walk or a Mexican walk, just a walk, or do that slither thing that your people do."

The men stood with locked eyes as more and more attorneys were returning to their seats at the conference table.

With all the restraint that he could possibly muster, Hamilton moved closer to the President, and spoke with a controlled voice.

"Stephon Clark was killed for standing while Black. Breanna Taylor was killed for sleeping while Black. Philando Castille was killed for sitting in his car while Black. And Jonathan Ferrell was killed for walking while Black right here in Charlotte."

"When this country starts treating Black people better, then we can discuss a variety. But right now Sir, it's Black Lives Matter and only Black Lives that Matter! So if speaking up for *'members of my family'* is going to be a problem for the white, racist assholes in this room, then fuck your firm. I am a DAMN GOOD ATTORNEY and can do a helluva lot better than take orders from a piece of shit like you."

"And that's white shit, in case you're confused by the color. Not Asian shit and not Hispanic shit. Just fucking white SHIT!"

Hamilton went to his office, grabbed his briefcase and walked to his car. He was too angry to drive, so he sat on the trunk of his car and allowed the sun to dry the tears that disobeyed his pleas to not fall.

15

················

MR. JEFFERRY BENJAMIN STICKLES trades stocks for *Wall Street Trophies*. The company was located in an upscale suburb of Charlotte called Ballantyne. The pressure was always on and performance was evaluated on a daily basis.

Greek was watching his trade monitors when another trader said "Yo Greek! The brothers want to see you in the head office."

He looked at his watch, and there were still fourteen minutes of trading left for the day. He usually cleared all of his stock positions five minutes before the closing bell. He thought to himself, *'fuck'em, they can wait.'*

At 4:25 pm, he initiated his routine and sold off all of his stock positions. Feeling proud of himself, he casually strolled to the head office.

He tapped the door several times and then barked, "Greek is in the HOUSE! Fellas, fellas, fellas!"

He looked into the stoic faces staring back at him.

"Why the long faces?" He clapped his hands several times. "Greek is in the HOUSE! Come on now, let's change the energy in this room."

He laughed then smiled.

Mike folded his arms across his chest as he spoke, "You're in a great mood considering you've lost over half a million dollars of our clients' money. Add to that, the fact that you've been insubordinate to the instructions of your Trade Supervisor over the past three months. You don't get to do whatever you want just because we're frat brothers. Rules are rules and we are trying to run a tight ship."

Greek finally took a seat between the two men. Looking back and forth at each one as he spoke, "Everyone has a bad run eventually. But four years ago...."

"GODDAMN GREEK!" Quinn shouted. "Why are you always living in the past? Four years ago was the last time you made this company any money. Three years ago you were second from last in performance. Last year you were the last in performance and RIGHT NOW you are the last in performance. Why didn't you short the Lee Rose Pharmaceutical stock? It's your industry. We had the inside scoop on that one and you FUCKED IT UP!"

"Shorting stocks goes against my personal philosophy of trading."

"Oh my god," Mike uttered, throwing his hands in the air. "No one gives two fucks about your personal, investment philosophy. We've had this conversation before. Your duty is to trade by OUR PHILOSOPHY, and fulfill your commitment as a fiduciary to our clients. Had you shorted the stock, we could be sitting on millions in commissions and transaction fees right now."

"Look, I placed the order for a put-option but never hit the button. I just..."

Mike felt sorry for the man, but didn't mince his words.

"You just thought about yourself instead of the company and instead of your clients."

Quinn waited for this moment and enjoyed every second.

"The rule is the person with the lowest rate of return at the end of the quarter gets fired. We've covered for you at our own detriment and against our own morals. Frat brother or not, we have to let you go. We cannot continue to treat you differently from the other employees."

Greek jumped to his feet and screamed, "I GOT SEVEN KIDS!"

He couldn't comprehend the backlash that came from his frat brothers.

"And a wife that's going to kick your ass, might I add," Quinn said. "Look, truth be told, I wanted to fire you last year, but everyone brought up your damn kids. Why didn't you think about your family and push the FUCKING BUTTON?"

Quinn rose to his feet to stare down Greek. The men traded breaths.

"HEY!" Mike called. "Back down Quinn. Quinn! I said back down."

Mike had dreaded this moment, but could no longer avoid it. Greek had repeatedly made the same mistakes, and blatantly disobeyed instructions.

Quinn returned to his seat.

"We're finally getting rid of your ass." He couldn't stop smiling.

"I know that I don't always follow instructions. And yes, I have lost some of our client's money, but this is Wall Street. Returns aren't guaranteed."

Greek stretched open his arms.

"Mike we've been down since college roommates. Please don't listen to Quinn."

Greek looked desperate to the man standing in front of him.

"And I've been carrying your Black ass on my back like a one-hundred and eighty pound, soaking wet sack of shit ever since. You stink up everywhere you go. I got you four different jobs before you came here, and the only reason you're here is because I own the company."

Mike threw his hands up, then dropped them.

"And Quinn is an equal co-founder who has never let me down."

"Ok, so I let you down. I get it. Ha, ha, ha, you scared me. I just need one more chance. Don't kick me out like this."

Greek stood in front of him with his hands in the prayer position, and his eyes were closed. He was moving his lips as if he spoke a silent prayer.

"You kicked yourself out. You're not just letting me down. Like it or not, you're letting Quinn down as well. That's something that I've taken into consideration, even more so than our friendship. This is business brother."

Mike dug into his jacket pocket, and pulled out a check.

"This is from Quinn and me. This is six months of your salary, minus any commissions or bonuses, and we are only doing this because of those kids."

Watching Greek make a mockery of praying, pissed Mike off even more. He brought both hands to his face, and rubbed his eyes forcefully. As if going temporarily blind would be better than looking at Greek.

Quinn barked out, "The only reason! I would love nothing more than to see your bitch ass walk out of here crying and broke."

Quinn was ecstatic with the moment. He looked and felt relieved. He had begged Mike to get rid of this guy for over a year. The man was planning his celebration when Mike snapped.

"JUST GET OUT OF HERE! Right now, get off your ass and get out of my office." He stared into the back of Quinn's head, as the man stood then paused to take another hard look into Greek's eyes before his exit.

Mike turned to take the seat where Quinn once sat. After four steps, he dropped into the sofa. He felt sorry for his friend.

A sudden smile crossed Greek's face.

"Remember that time at FAMU when...."

"STOP!" Mike held a hand up, with his head down shaking from side-to-side.

"I don't want to remember any more times at FAMU," he continued. "That was over twenty years ago. We are in our forties. The decisions we make today have many more consequences than the decisions we made as kids. When are you going to make the decision to grow up? GREEK! YOU HAVE TO GROW UP! GREEK! GREEK! CAN YOU HEAR ME?"

Greek awoke in his bed and stared at the ceiling. He anticipated the singing of the alarm clock. He raised his head to look at his wife, who was sound asleep. Then he rolled on his side to turn off the alarm.

Greek was fired six months ago, but still left the house as if he had a job. He sat at the edge of the bed. He felt the movement of his wife as the mattress rose like a seesaw. She touched his back to comfort him.

Greek jumped out of bed, "DON'T TOUCH ME! DON'T FUCKING TOUCH ME! Even your fucking fingers are FAT!" He looked bewildered at his wife.

She simply rolled over.

"I'm not starting my day like this with you." She pulled the sheet over her head.

Greek took a shower and got dressed. Before he walked out of the bedroom, he spoke in his wife's direction.

"Watch the news okay. Just watch the fucking news."

His wife pulled the sheet down but maintained her gaze on the ceiling.

"For REAL this time? I mean FOR REAL, FOR REAL THIS TIME?"

Greek went to the garage and sat in his car. He could never tell his wife that he had gotten fired again. He had disappointed her too many times. He would rather die than face that woman with another *'Baby I got fired but it wasn't my fault story.'*

Anything would be better than that.

ANYTHING!

16

I WAS IN my office with my Executive Assistant, Kadijah, when Greek walked in.

I gave him the head nod and kept working. After Kadijah finished taking notes, she told smiled.

"Have fun at the spa" she said.

Greek interrupted our interaction with "You should come with us, that way I can save some damn money." He looked the young lady up and down with his tongue out.

Kadijah winked at me, before walking toward the door without an glance at Greek, "If I go, I'm charging much more than those skanks at the spa," she said. "So I would NOT help your wallet."

She showed me love with her daily salute.

"Thank you for the knowledge but I really love the wisdom."

Greek laughed.

"Yo that's cute!" he yelled at a closed door. Then with a louder yell, "WHERE MY SALUTE! Come on Bro, you told her to say that?"

"You're Greek and I'm Knowledge for a reason," I said. "We have symbolic code names for a very specific purpose Mr. Stickles. Mr. Jefferry Benjamin Stickles!"

"Not my whole government name. Bro, I'll be quiet. Please. Just call me Greek. Damn!"

He shook violently like a wet dog; as if his government name could be shaken off.

"We are on the plantation," I reminded him. By this time, I put on my jacket suit and we dapped up.

Greek gave me something to gnaw on as we walked toward my office door to exit.

"Ever since the last shooting, brothers and sisters have been talking about a 'Black Out.' This, from my understanding, is one day out of the year that all Blacks unite and commit to not spend one dollar in this country. What do you think about that?"

I heard his question but he knew I wouldn't respond until we left the building. There were too many ears to start the discussion inside of the building. We walked to an elevator that always seemed to be full of people going places instead of working. I always waited until we turned the corner to utter my retort.

"I think I smell opportunity. Why not expand that to say let's *'Black Out and Black Up.'* Instead of not spending one Black dime, let's truly boycott the corporate plantation and only buy Black period. And then we expand that to Black Up once per month. Why do we have to wait until the next shooting or the one after that or the one after that to illustrate our power with Black dollars? We should be doing this on a regular monthly basis until we can do it on a weekly basis until the habit is a habit and we do it on a daily basis. Either that or we create our own *'Black digital currency'* that operates external to white economics. Now that would utterly destroy this country. See how fast the ABC's come after us then........ FBI..... CIA....IRS..... hell, even the YMCA doesn't like too many of us in the building at the same time!"

I laughed.

"Do you know how hard it is to get ten Blacks to agree on anything? You're talking about...." Greek gave me an exaggerated look of despair.

"Don't come at me with negativity about my people. You know damn well we are the only race in this country that doesn't have the right to unite. We united post slavery; they stole everything from us to set us back. We united in Tulsa, OK and they dropped bombs from airplanes. We united in Wilmington, NC and they killed our people, stole our houses, stole and divided up our money in our bank accounts and then stole and divided up our land that we accumulated since post slavery and, once again, set us back. Multiply everything I've said ten times in every state in American't and tell the truth. And the truth is that Black people are not citizens and when we try to unite the white folks send in the ABC's to infiltrate, neutralize, and mitigate any possible positive collusion. So don't blame us, reach us and teach us. But let's use this as an opportunity to form a nonprofit and roll with '*Black Out.*'

I held out my hand.

"We can do this. I'll write it all up and get the fellas together for a presentation and further discussion to let everyone drop their two cents in. I had a conversation before with Brains about establishing our own Black digital currency. And he loved it!"

"Nah, fuck that." He pushed my hand away and kept walking. "You're talking about a dark place. Like the dimples in my wife's ass, I can't see the bottom."

Greek shuffled faster to move ahead of me.

I couldn't.

"Is this you changing the subject after my Black-on-Black, philosophical epiphany of the perfect '*pro-Black people non-profit?*'"

"You scared me when you brought up the ABCs." Greek started looking in different directions as if we might be followed. "Listen Negro, there is no one better at neutralizing a race than the ABCs. I might not be able to put my name on that list; I owe the IRS some money,"

"Of course there's no one better, especially when the FBI and CIA have been practicing on Black people since the invention of white people."

I stopped speaking, realizing that I was about to broach a subject better suited for Nice Head or Big Brains.

"And that's why we are changing the subject to my wife's weight."
I laughed again.

"Last night, she was punching me in the stomach with her fore-head and I had an epiphany–for the last eleven years I have been fucking ghost pussy."

Greek was straight-faced with no chaser. He held up a hand.

"My fat ass wife put on some lingerie for me, right. First of all, I didn't even know they made lingerie for fat bitches but anyway. She does this spin around in front of me and then stops and smiles and began walking toward me with the expectation of sex. My dick could not get hard to save my life but what I realized is that I had to go back in the day reminiscing to when she was two hundred pounds smaller and when I use to be able to pick her ass up and pretzel fuck her. My point is this, in order to fuck the present pussy I have to think about the ghost pussy that use to be fun. Today I got a three hundred pound goat standing in front of me but I want what I use to have, the hundred pound tiger."

I was stunned.

"If you have a question, permission has been granted."

"How long have you been married now?" I asked.

"Going on nineteen years," Greek responded.

"At what point does this amazing, highly intelligent sister, who carried your ass through college by the way, always had a job, even when you didn't by the way, gave you seven children by the way, nursed you back from death when you had cancer by the way, get to gain weight? She's your fucking wife and you have seven amazing children from this woman. How could you possibly think or demand that she keeps her figure from college?"

"Easy. And I want the figure from high school, not college, because that's where we met." Greek uttered selfishly.

"Please tell me this is the one time that you are not serious." I stated. "It's not fair to place that kind of demand on Petra. I mean fo' real, fo' real, outta all the brothers, your wife has all of the char-acteristics that I would want in a wife. Of course I don't know her like you do, but I just can't fathom falling in love to stop loving because of weight. After delivering to you those beautiful daughters. You are wrong Greek. I've had your back on many occasions, but not this one."

"Not only am I serious, serious, I'm also seriously selfish by the way. I don't want an obese wife, man. Remember in college; go back to the first time that I introduced her to you. Pure chocolate with a body like Florence Griffith Joyner."

Greek looked to the sky and with his hands; he rotated each one back and forth to his lips, blowing kisses to the sky. Then he continued.

"She kept her size until baby number five. I mean what the fuck; we only had two more children."

He stopped talking and stared at me.

"You're a hypocritical asshole you know that. You're judging me right now with that dumbass look on your face, but why aren't you married Mr. Smarty Pants? You're supposed to have all the knowledge but you're still single, and why? Because you bounce off the ass TEN TIMES, and then create a false imperfection as an excuse to say that *'she wasn't the one.'* Where the fuck are your kids and perfect wife? As a matter of fact, you got so much fucking knowledge you probably can perform the abortions yourself by now."

We locked eyes at that statement. It was rare that Greek could say something that chained my mouth and throat. I couldn't talk and the spit somehow evaporated, creating a desert on my tongue. He made me feel empty in this moment.

Greek smiled and tried to revert back to joking. "Now move out of the way so that I can get ignorant in this spa and make it about me, as usual, by the way."

I couldn't move and wasn't shit funny right now. I twirled the faces of the last ten, twenty, thirty, and more women, through my mind. Was not one of them the right one? Or was it me? I couldn't move, so Greek moved around me, pulled out his member card and ran it from top to bottom in the center of the door. A light flashed, the door hummed and he entered.

We went into the spa and were escorted by a beautiful sister into another room where twelve women, completely naked stood holding numbers.

"You do know that it's my turn to pick first, right?" Greek asked without looking at me, focused on the women.

"You say that same bullshit every time we come here." I looked to the ceiling and shook my head. I tried to push the past out of the way so that I could enjoy my present.

Greek fucked it up. Greek fucked me up. Now I had to wonder, 'how many kids would I have had right now if none of those girls agreed to the abortions?' Greek's laughter and loud slap of his hands snatched me back to reality. The first abortion was the first girl I fucked at FAMU. Greek acted as if nothing happened before we walked in here. As if he didn't just reproof my ego and toss that shit in a blender.

Greek smiled and turned his back to the women.

"My apologies if I kicked you in the vagina bro. But you have to get off that Petra shit until you get your own damn kids, your own damn wife, and she gain two-hundred plus on your ass. Then we can talk."

He completed a dance spin that was crazy corny, but made me laugh.

I pushed the Tallahassee abortion clinic out of my head. I high stepped and jumped in front of him, causing him to run into my back and then we both laughed.

Continuing my stride in front of him, I said, "I'm always in the mood for chocolate and double chocolate; numbers 4 and 8 please."

The young ladies smiled and made their way over to me. I placed an arm around each waist and began walking to the back.

I spoke over my shoulder, "And we're each paying for our own services Mr. Selfish." I didn't even wait to see what numbers he chose.

I understood Greek's definition of seeing ghost pussy, but I'd rather see ghost pussy than the unborn, ghost babies, that I hear crying when I wake sometimes, in the middle of the night.

Chapter Sixteen

Ninety minutes later, with the weight of the world off my shoulders, I was hungry. The Spa had finger foods but they never gave you enough to actually get full. Greek walked out with a smile about two minutes later. I had forgiven my brother because that's what brothers do. We dapped up and walked out of the building. I was in a zone. Thinking and not thinking at the same time. Just happy to be alive. Just happy to have a job. Just happy to be single.

I wanted to discuss Greek's marriage but I figured I'd wait until over lunch. I forgave him but was prepared for a comeback. I wanted a second chance at our verbal jousting. "Where are we eating?" I asked.

"I know you want something close, but there's a spot over the bridge that I found and want to take you to."

"Come on bro, you should've told me that before I left the office. I told them I was coming back. If we cross that bridge, it's a wrap after that."

"Boss man! Just call the office and cancel the rest of the day. You don't smash two bitches and go back to work. Massa' will understand your plight. Call and tell'em your sac and stomach empty. And it's a universal law that one of them needs to be full," he laughed.

"What is your boss going to do; make you eat her?"

"Alright Bro, I'll call once we get to where we're going."

"And that's why you're the boss MAN! Let me walk ahead of you and make this call."

There are moments in your life where things will happen that don't make any scientific sense. And you will replay those moments over and over trying to deduce the sequence of events leading up to that serendipitous flash that scarred your reality.

He came to my office. We talked like the best friends we were. We went and got some ass. We were on our way to eat. I didn't want to go where he suggested. I gave in anyway. We were halfway across the bridge. He said that he wanted to walk ahead of me to make a phone call. And then he jumped off the bridge.

17

·················

THE POLICE OFFICER repeatedly asked me the same questions; rephrased but the same. However, in my mind I was tried to gather my own questions. I also tried to maintain loyalty to a deceased friend, when I couldn't understand why he was even deceased. Did I miss something? Am I the world's dumbest, best friend?

"Sir, I need you to focus for me," the Police Officer kept demanding. "If you could just answer my questions please, and then we both can move on to something else."

I needed to go back to the Spa first thing tomorrow, and get that charge removed from his credit card and placed on mine. I doubted he let his wife see his credit card bills. I didn't want things to become worse than what they will already be. He left behind a wife and seven kids.

"Sir, where did the two of you go after you left your office?"

"I answered that question."

The Overseer shot back, "No you didn't."

"We were walking and talking, but he and I could start debating and end up standing in one spot for hours going back and forth before we started walking again. It was just part of the fun being together. We disagreed on almost everything."

I rubbed the back of my head.

"It could take us an hour to cross the street; especially during playoffs!"

"You smell like liquor, where did the two of you go to get drinks from?"

"I don't know. I wasn't paying attention. We were debating. Next thing I know I got hungry and he said that he knew a spot across the bridge. I really can't do this right now. He has a wife and seven kids. I need to go talk to his wife. I don't want one of your guys getting there before me. Please."

He stared at me for what seemed like a day, then the Overseer handed me his card.

"Tomorrow," he said, "you better find me before I find you. Get your shit together and tell me the truth. You didn't kill him, we know that. Over a hundred people saw him jump. So why lie?"

"Because friends are worth lying for."

I turned away from the cop and looked out over the bridge.

"Even when their dead. Some shit is actually supposed to die with them."

I ordered a Lyft. I crossed the street and leaned my back against a building. The weight of the world was back on my shoulders.

The driver wanted to talk, but after I told him, *'my best friend just committed suicide,'* he looked worse than I did. When we got to Greek's house, I exited the car feeling guilty.

I've known Greek and Petra since the beginning of life at FAMU. When someone uses the term, strong, Black woman, I think of her before my own mother. I was shocked that Greek felt such shame for his wife because of her weight. I also felt he was wrong, but that didn't matter now. Walking to his front door from the driveway was the longest walk of my life. Football fields seemed shorter. In actuality, it was probably less than twenty feet.

Before I made it up the porch stairs, his oldest daughter, Patra, burst through the front door to greet me.

"UNCLE!" She smiled.

With a heavy heart, I wasn't ready to talk and still tried not to breakdown. I gave her a tight squeeze and grumbled. She used both hands to hold my right hand as I opened the storm door with my left. Petra's eyes looked at me as if she already knew. She shook her head side-to-side before I even spoke.

"Can you tell the girls to go to their rooms while we talk please?"

Petra thundered, "GIRLS! BRING YO ASSES IN HERE!"

I wondered why strong, Black women always did the opposite of what Black men asked. I was completely thrown off guard.

"That's the opposite of what I asked you."

I raised my arms and slapped them against my sides.

"I'm raising girls to be young ladies and young ladies to be women. I don't hide anything from them because it's too damn much on that television and even more on that nasty ass internet. Between my reality and reality TV, there is absolutely nothing that you can say that they haven't already heard or going to hear one day from a NICKEL like you."

All seven daughters were gathered around their mother staring at me; ages 17, 15, and 13 standing behind the couch where their mother sat, and the younger four, 10, 8, 6 and 3, all sitting to her left.

"There is a reason your father is not here and he is about to tell you. It might be a lie or it might be the truth. Whatever the reason I just want all of you to remember one thing; this is the man that helps your father cheat on me. This is the man that your father calls his best friend. The same man that was the best man at our wedding, and at the hospital when each one of you were born. He is also the same man that, even though he knows that your father is fucking other women, he will walk in my house with a smile on his face and give me the biggest hug in the world.

"This is what men do for their 'BEST FRIENDS!' I want y'all to remember that and listen to whatever silliness about to come out of his mouth so that you can hear the sincerity in his voice. Get past the love and kindness in it and listen to everything that he isn't saying. Because when a Black man speaks, he always speaking twice; saying shit he wants you to be dumb enough to believe and then holding silent shit in that he think you too dumb to figure out."

The two oldest daughters began laughing then coughed and covered their mouths. They never took their eyes off of me but the youngest entertained themselves watching spots on the floor.

"I wanted to walk in here and be strong, loving and supportive. But now I just got the answer to my biggest question. If I had to come home to a nasty bitch like you, I would've killed myself too. As a matter of fact, NOW, I don't even understand why he didn't kill himself sooner. FUCK YOU PETRA! He's your husband. Whatever issues the two of you had, the two of you HAD. YOU DON'T TELL YOUR FUCKING CHILDREN AND TURN THEM AGAINST THEIR FATHER!"

She rose slowly off the couch; three hundred pounds can only rise slowly. Part of me wanted to storm out of the house and part of me still had questions. I still had questions. He was still my best friend.

"Look at my daughters. LOOK AT THEM! You walk in my house and don't even know what is going on in my house, but you're concerned about what my girls hear. Every day for the last two years, Jefferry would wake up, eat breakfast and then look me right in my face and say today is the day that I'm going to kill myself. Watch the news baby. And then the next day and then the next day and then the next day. Do you have any idea what it's like living with a man who tells you that every day; and his girls."

She covered her face with her hands. Then raised them to the ceiling.

"I'm not crying for that evil, sack of a Satan shit stain," Petra said to me. "Telling me wasn't enough for Jefferry, about six months ago he started telling his daughters, today daddy is killing himself, it'll be on the news when you get home from school. Do you have any idea of the psychological damage this man has done to me and these girls that you're so concerned about? Did you know that he was doing this to us? Did he ever brag about this to you?"

She walked toward me, her hands on her hips.

"Did Mr. Stickles get his dick wet before he died? I mean since you so concerned about the girls, why don't you give us more detail so that we can gauge how concerned their father was before he left us? Or committed suicide? I mean, wait, is he outside in the bushes? Where is Jefferry?"

Petra leaned to the side with a wide smile and stared at me. His daughters seemed void of any emotion. They were prepared for this and I was the one surprised. Her face seemed demonic. I'd seen that look before, the look of marriage.

"He came by the office and we were walking to get something to eat. He told me that he knew of a new place across the bridge that he wanted me to try. He said that he needed to make a phone call and sped up ahead of me. Next thing I know, when we got midway across the bridge he jumped."

"Doing that long walk, I'm sure the two of you spoke of something." Her eyes ended the sentence with a question mark.

"Yeah, he told me that he had an epiphany about something called ghost pussy. But he kept laughing and was rambling. He played around so much; I never got the explanation that I was waiting for."

She turned to face her daughters and waved a finger in the air.

"Do y'all hear how he mixes his lies with his truths? Half of everything he's saying is real and half of everything he's saying is a Goddamn lie."

She turned to me again.

"Why do you think lying is helping Jefferry? Everyone in this room knows what ghost pussy is and I know damn well that he told you before he did what he did. That man was mean and nasty and hurtful. So let me share a story of the deceased with you now that Mr. GREEK!"

Petra laughed.

"I mean since your boy is gone. I gave him seven kids and yes, I gained weight but this is the same weight that I've had since baby girl number three. And if you look around the room, we did not stop fucking after number three was born; but things change. I got sexy for my boo one night and wanted to bless him with my essence and he told me no. He told me that the only way he would touch me was if I went and got a picture made of the smaller me, blow up the face and tape it over mine and maybe."

A long silence hung in the air.

"And he meant 'MAYBE' his dick would get hard. We have done all kind of kinky. We even evented some shit. So instead of taking it as a slap in the face, I just threw it in the kinky file. After all, it was still my face that he wanted to see. So I did it. If that's what my husband wanted, then I would do it."

"But Jefferry is Jefferry and even that didn't last. The next thing I know he starts asking me where his ghost pussy at? The smaller me. The me before the kids. The me he fell in love with. There is only so much I can do for my husband and nothing more. At some point my husband has to love me for me. NO MATTER WHAT! TIL DEATH DO US THE FUCK A PART OR ONE OF US FUCKING DIES! Now that motherfucker is dead, and I'm here with seven girls that are going to be young ladies that are going to be women. Whatever man they allow themselves to love and marry, they will learn from me, to demand to be loved and respected. Now what else have you done to help lie for Jefferry?"

I raised and dropped my shoulders.

"There's nothing else Petra. But if Jefferry had a mental illness why wouldn't you tell me? We, you and I, could have gotten him help."

"You really don't get it do you?"

I looked at her emotionless daughters with no tears. No shock. I looked back at Petra and shrugged my shoulders again.

"Get what?"

"You have to have a mental illness to get married."

Their ten year old daughter, Jalita, spoke, "Momma can I ask a question?"

Petra nodded at the child.

"Uncle you didn't answer my mother's question about our father. Did you help him cheat on her with other women?"

"Your mother didn't ask me a question she made an indictment; an accusation. It's a statement that you throw at someone with or without proof. In this particular argument your mother has zero proof and is just upset right now about what has been going on. Your mother didn't marry me, she married your father. And if mommy really thought that your father was cheating it is because of decisions that he made on his own. However, since you asked and I never want to be like one of those mean Black men that your mommy referenced earlier, I will tell you and all of your sisters that I have never, once, ever, never never never never been asked, or voluntarily offered to help your father cheat on your mother. He is a grown man, older than me and if that is a decision that he wanted to make, he did not need my advice, counsel or permission. Thank you for that wonderful question!"

"GET YOUR ASS OUT OF MY HOUSE!" Petra shouted at me, disgusted.

"I didn't know what I expected, but I didn't expect this." I felt ashamed of myself.

"Good. And don't expect to come to the funeral. We do not want you there. He may not have asked you, but you knew. You always knew, and you're a fucking liar. You're just like every other Nickel that graduated from FAMU; mentally stuck on the set trying to fuck everything that moves. You brag about graduating from an HBCU, '*BLACK ON BLACK EVERYTHING*' but how much of your paycheck goes back to FAM to help those that followed you there? You wear the most expensive suits."

She looked me up and down.

"You wear the most expensive shoes, and drink the most expensive liquor, but you're just covering your cheap ass soul. I WISH, I REALLY WISH THE TWO OF YOU WOULD HAVE HELD HANDS AND JUMPED TOGETHER! Because as long as you're alive you will continue to represent everything that's Jefferry. A coward, A FUCKING COWARD that is so scared of white men that you can't fight, you come home to a Black woman that you can abuse. You always abuse HER! You abuse everything that Black women represent; and do you know what that is?"

"No Petra, please tell me."

"Respect and responsibility!" She had her head raised high, with her hands on her hips. Eyes wide arresting me with fury.

"But you weren't married to me. There were no vows to me. I didn't owe you..."

"YOU OWED ME RESPECT GODDAMNIT!!! I know who you are, and you don't have to marry bullshit to smell that it's bullshit because BULLSHIT stinks wherever it goes. NOW GET THE FUCK OUT OF MY HOUSE!!!"

She sat back in her original seat on the couch and hugged her daughters. She was breathing heavy.

"We want to watch the news and see Daddy on the news. Now that he finally did what he has been telling us he was going to do for the last two DAMN years."

18

I SAT IN my office the next day. The idea of taking time off was too much; I didn't want to be alone. Knowing that I was not going to be allowed at the funeral was killing me. I was inept but my office gave me a certain comfort. Even though I sat there by myself, I knew there were people on the other side of the door. The intermittent noise I heard, kept my grief at bay.

I got so many phone calls that morning I turned my cellphone off. I got tired of explaining and re-explaining just to have to explain and re-explain again about what Greek did or why he did it. I didn't have any answers. I read through emails and made an attempt at busy work.

Lava entered the office, fell back against the door and folded her arms across her chest.

"You shouldn't be here."

"I'm scared to be alone. And it's not like I can go on a vacation and actually enjoy myself. I'd rather be here."

I watched her contemplating. She was pensive and then she wasn't. Decision made. Without saying anything further, she came over and gave me a long hug. It felt great. It felt needed. I felt needed.

Since she possessed pussy power, I never tried to motion toward sex. That was hers to control. I would just always go along. Plus, she was hard to read. I never knew when she did or didn't want things to go further than a hug. So for her I was sexually submissive.

She whispered, "I know what you need," and unbuckled my belt.

She nibbled softly on my neck and stroked me. She pulled at my tie, choked me and stared intently into my eyes. She toyed with me; stroked fast then slow then fast and then slow again. She bit at my chest, worked her way down to my stomach, and placed her head below my waist. It must have been all of the emotions since the suicide the previous day, because I came hard and fast. I don't even know if her tongue ever touched me.

I slid out of my chair and onto my knees so that we could be face-to-face. I pecked her on the forehead, pulled my shirt down and then laid on the floor, pants still to my ankles. I was drained.

I closed my eyes and spoke. I told her everything from the moment Greek came to my office, to him jumping, to the police questioning, to the confrontational battle with his wife, and the un-invitation to the funeral. I felt her get up and I heard her moving around the office. I felt her hands with a wet wipe cleaning me up.

"Raise up," she said as she slid my pants back into place.

My eyes were still closed as the scenes from yesterday came and went. Lava told me to get up, fix my clothes, and sit in my chair. I remained submissive to her.

"First of all, I still don't think that you should be here. I mean, this is the one time that I would have broken my rule to come to your home. I would have checked on you."

"I don't believe that."

"Too bad," she pouted. Secondly, when Greek's wife made the analogy of marriage and mental illness, I don't think she meant, literally, that you had to have a mental illness. My deduction of that statement is that when you're in love you become obsessed with another human being, to the point that people may view you as crazy. Like 'crazy in love' or 'looking so crazy right now.'

"Ok Beyonce."

"Seriously! You two were in a high, emotional state. I'm sure that's what she would say if you could get her to elaborate. You'd just told her that her husband died, she had to be in some form of shock. Or if things were really bad, she could have even been emotionally relieved to some degree."

"So what does it mean when you stop looking crazy?"

I held up a hand to stop her from answering.

"And would you be relieved if you found out right now, in this moment, that your husband was dead?"

Lava dropped her head then raised it, looking at me with one eye.

"You're going to keep doing this aren't you?" She ran her fingers through her hair, "The honeymoon high is real. But like any other high it simply can't last forever. You can still be in love, but I think the goal is to not allow routine to damage the relationship. You have to keep it spicy and maintain constant communication."

"So am I spicy, and do you communicate what we do to your husband?"

Lava didn't blink or flinch, "I tell him everything about you."

"I actually believe that for some reason. Most of the time when you mention him I think every word out of your mouth is a damn lie. Just your way of seeking justification to sit in my lap. But this has a strange sense of truth to it. I'd actually like to meet your husband now."

"You don't have to believe anything that I say on a personal note if that makes you feel better."

"Do you know what *reverse ninja my shit* means because you didn't answer my second question?"

"Besides, at the end of the day we are co-workers, and I am your boss. So believe what your boss says, and that's what's the most important."

"If he died right now would it change anything between us?"

"First you want to meet him and now you want him dead. The fact that your being morbid is a very strong indication that you need to take your Black ass home and grieve like normal humans."

"And you're being evasive and trying to reverse ninja my shit."

"I only reverse ninja with my husband. Sorry, but you're not that important to me."

She spun around on one foot and rose up a finger.

"FUN YES..... but not that important. After all, this is a SIT-U-ATION-SHIP, not a Goddamn relationship."

"You're trying to hijack the conversation and turn it back to morbidity because you want me to feel WHAT LAVA? ANSWER MY FUCKING QUESTION PLEASE! Hit the ninja pause button and act like a woman one time for me; a woman with some type of emotion."

"The answer doesn't matter because if my husband died right now, I, like regular humans, would take a few weeks off to grieve his absence and plan my future. Would that include you, probably not."

"Then fuck it, let's not wait for him to die, just leave him."

"I didn't want you to be the one to fire the gay guy. I tried to have someone else do it, but the powers that be thought that you would be the most efficient, given your propensity to lack empathy. The same propensity that made you ideal to FUCK!"

I laughed. The energy between us became uncontrollable. I had asked a question and didn't like the response. I walked around the office to give myself time to get my emotions in check.

"Ok," I said. Now I definitely know that you are trying to reverse ninja the conversation."

I walked over and stood directly in front of her. When I raised my hands to touch her face, she turned around and walked away from me.

"Empathy is exactly what I need right now. I realize that no love is a perfect love. But..."

"Please shut up..... like I'm trying not to vomit right now. If you keep talking you're going to ruin our office fling. You're fun, and that's it. Not husband material. Not serious material. Just fun material. You watched your best friend commit suicide and it has you feeling some type of way. I get it. Now all of a sudden you love me. Leave my husband. Come to you. Stay with you and then one day you wake up and you're back to being you and then...?"

She threw her hands up and then she slid them down the side of her hips.

"You start fucking someone else at the office?" she asked. "Or maybe you just lose interest and tell me to get out because you realized that you made a mistake, and sorry for ruining my life but you were in an emotional state and not really thinking. I'm not going to let myself fall for this SHIT!"

I sat back in my chair with my feet crossed on my desk watching her intensely. I wanted to speak, but she raised her voice as she continued.

"OR BETTER YET! I come running to you and say *'baby I love you'* and then you reverse ninja my shit and, instead of saying I love you back, you start talking about your invisible Pitbull that needs to go for a walk because he needs air!"

"What if the honeymoon is never over for us?"

"And what if it is? I get it okay."

She stood in front of my desk.

"There is a certain excitement that comes from fucking in the office that I can't give you fucking at home in a normal bed. So what do we do? Fuck at the movies? Restaurant bathroom? Backseat of my car? I'm scared because I don't believe that you know what you're saying in this moment, and I have already thought about this because I knew one day your dumbass might actually think that you loved me."

She turned her back to me and folded her arms across her chest.

"I can't match this level of excitement for the rest of my life. And it would drive me bonkers if I even positioned myself to try. It's not me that you love. It's the *'fucking in the office high'* that you get that you love........and the thought of the door opening. The what-if we get caught adrenalin in your veins is what you love. It has nothing to do with me."

She turned around again, arms still folded.

"Did you know that sometimes my husband conducts business in this building?"

"I think you're right, but no, I didn't."

Her face was stoic.

"Sometimes I think that I want to get caught." She began shaking her head. "I don't know why I'm telling you this, but thank you for that."

"I think I should've stayed home, but since I'm here, BOSS!" I waited for our eyes to meet before I spoke, "Can you please leave the office that I like to believe is mine?"

She opened her mouth and placed her hands on her hips. It looked like she was debating whether to cuss me out or not. Decision made. She dropped her hands, walked toward the door, shaking her head all the way out.

I felt like shit. I'm on an emotional roller coaster but still didn't want to be alone.

I called Lu Ling to see if my father was sitting outside of his restaurant. After a few minutes, he came back to the phone and said no. I decided to clear my head and work for a few hours. At least my work loved me back.

19

....

I WANTED TO stop crying but my eyes kept with tears at the mental image of Greek jumping off the bridge. My mind travelled from one situation I couldn't control, to another my father.

He chose to be homeless because marriage to my mother caged him so drastically, that the mere thought of being behind four walls causes anxiety.

"There's something my father isn't telling me," I said out loud.

A little girl tugged at my shirt, I wasn't sure how long she'd been there. I blinked several times and saw her mother pointing.

I look down into the most precious eyes.

"Don't cry," the little girl said. She handed me a napkin and I smiled larger than I can remember. I knelt down to her level.

"Thank you for making me smile."

I took the napkin and she ran back to her mother sitting down.

"He's going to stop crying now mommy."

I removed my glasses and realized, for the first time, that I'm actually on a subway. I had no recollection of getting on. I placed my wet napkin in my right jacket pocket and put my glasses on.

I exit the subway with the rush of humans, all running off to do nothing somewhere, just so they can say that they are busy when they get there, and then rush to somewhere else and do more nothing.

As soon as I walked into corporate, I feel the energy change.

Like I know that something is about to happen, but of course, I just don't know what exactly. The security guards appear to be avoiding my gaze. No head nods or smiles and comments about the game last night. I keep looking in their direction because I'm sure they saw me.

Something was up.

The security guards spoke to everyone, every day.

I stepped onto the elevator, removed my glasses and closed my eyes. I reminded myself that I was at work; to stop thinking about my father and get my crap together. All personal issues were required to be left outside of the building. Work was for work.

I opened my eyes, placed my glasses on the bridge of my nose and hit the button for the eighth floor. There was more silence, as I walked down the aisle leading to my office. Everyone feigned busy.

Oh boy, I think I saw this movie before. When I got to my office the door was closed and the door was never closed unless I was on the other side of it, and I wanted it shut. I placed my right hand on the door knob and took a deep breath.

After witnessing Greek jump, I may have needed a mental health check. I just wasn't ready to voice that to anyone.

To my delight, when I opened the door, Mr. Lamour sat at my desk. To his left stood my nemesis, office freak, and Human Resource Director, Lavana Rosa Cabrera.

She stood with her arms across her chest, face emotionless. We made eye contact but she never blinked and she never looked away. She looked more beautiful than ever, and that's what I hated about her. No matter how good or bad she treated me, the woman was all power; the dangerous kind, with beauty.

I walked over to my desk, casually counting the number of bodies in the room. I see two of the biggest security guards that I ever saw in my life. I didn't even know they worked here. I suddenly wondered if they were hired for the occasion.

My mentor and sometimes friend, and founder of the plantation stood, greeted me with a smile and head nod.

"Come on in and close the door behind you please. Do you know why you're here?"

"I'm here because this is my office, and that's my line by the way."

"Not today and not in this moment or any other moment after this day. Please sit the company briefcase on my desk and remove any of your personal items that may be in there. I will also need your badge and any keys in your possession that go to any door of this building. After you have complied, I have some questions for you and then we will discuss your termination, your vacation time on the books, your severance package and whether or not there will be a positive or negative referral for you from this office."

My mind said move. My feet wanted to move. My body thought it was moving. But nothing moved. It was a scary movie scene, where my boss, the desk and Human Resource Director all moved towards me in this slow and dramatic fashion. I felt my body collapse inward and I jumped as my boss's hands slammed the desk and he screamed.

"THIS ISN'T A FUCKING STARING CONTEST!"

I wanted to speak but some imaginary asshole poured a bucket of sand in my mouth, and I felt an utter dryness of tongue that prevented me from creating any saliva. I willed the power to walk forward to the desk, and as I got closer to it, the body guards got closer to me; until there was one on each side of me.

Mrs. Cabrera took a step forward, uncrossed her arms and placed her left hand on her hip, and her right hand on the desk. She leaned forward and spoke.

"The last time that I was in your office, I specifically asked you if you remembered whether or not Mr. Keon Patience told you that *'his husband was going to kill him.'* You answered in the negative and confidently stated that he did not. I would like to bring to your attention that the company is being sued. Mr. Keon Patience's body was found yesterday, along with his husband. However, it appeared that, not only was he confident that he would be killed for losing his job, he also took the pleasure of writing a letter to the Rainbow Association and mailing a copy to this office prior to his death. We really need you to read this letter."

If she was trying to be stern and forceful, it was the sexiest stern and forceful I've ever seen. Lucky me. If only Mr. Lamour wasn't in the office right now.

Just then, Mr. Lamour interrupted Lava and my carnal thoughts.

"Give that to me."

Without taking his eyes off of me, he raised his left hand and waited for the feel of the envelope. He then began tapping the envelope on his desk.

"Ten years of outstanding service and I can't think of one missed step by you; my favorite mentee by far. But my fucking hands are tied when gay associations get involved and start using phrases like *homophobic, gay-bashing, sexual preference, discrimination* and any other twinkle-toe bullshit that makes them twirl in their panties. Had he not mailed that letter, business would be business, and you would be sitting in this chair. But the gay hounds are barking and barking loud. I have to feed them someone and you volunteered the very moment that you didn't protect the gay guy."

The dryness of my mouth finally dissipated.

"Every married man that I have ever terminated screams '*my wife is going to kill me*,' so what makes this case different? Why should he get secret service protection when this wouldn't have been an issue if he were married to a woman?"

I made eye contact with Lava.

"And you never asked me that. You never asked me any questions pertaining to Mr. Patience receiving death threats from his husband."

She held my stare but didn't speak.

"Lesson number 44, young grasshopper. Your career will end over a fuck up, an alleged fuck up, or an '*if*' that leads to a major fuck up!"

As Mr. Lamour spoke, he nonchalantly walked over to the bar that used to be mine and made three drinks. One of the body guards rushed over to grab two of the drinks. He came back and handed me one and then walked over to the Human Resource Director to hand her one.

Lamour swallowed his scotch in one go, and motioned for the security guard to make him a new one. With his second drink in hand, he began his soliloquy.

"Gays possess power. A lot of it. And there are a lot of fucking gays in this city. They want rights. They want equality. They want every fucking thing; and deservedly so. They are Americans and we all know that Americans are greedy fuckers. If you have a problem with gays, then you have a problem with a lot of people. And when those people find out, an example has to be made. That example cannot be this company. It can be you. It will be you. But it cannot be MY company."

"When you heard Mr. Patience state that his husband would kill him," Lava started. "Did you laugh or smirk, or make any demeaning gesture that illustrated your hatred of gay men?"

First, she lied about our conversation, and now she's stamping me homophobic before I could even respond.

"Was your lack of reporting his concerns of being killed by his husband due to some issues of homophobia that you possess internally, and you finally got an opportunity to possibly and indirectly lead a male homosexual to his death?"

Lava sneered at me while retrieving back to her power pose; arms crossed over her chest, head high, and shoulders back.

I ignored the scowl on her face.

"You can say whatever makes you feel good, or whatever you need to say to make it easier on you to fire me, but it wasn't that."

Perplexed, Lava snapped, "But it wasn't what?"

"But it wasn't anything that you are saying. Did y'all practice this shit before I got here?"

I became irritated at the thought of being accused of something that I wasn't; homophobic. I actually had gay associates, but that would be a moot point, so I kept that information to myself.

I swore I heard Lava growl before she yelled.

"But it wasn't what? You appear to be having difficulty saying the word gay or homophobia. But it wasn't what? Elaborate!"

She is so damn good at ignoring my responses.

"I don't have to say the fucking word because none of the fucking words that you are using describe me. You are simply trying to implicate me in something that I had no control over. AND-IF-I-DID think he was in fear for his life, I would have made every recommendation possible to protect HIM-FROM-HIS-HUSBAND!"

I yelled back in her direction.

"And that's where you fucked up. If he was a she you would have done your job. But he was a he and you failed to do so. I think it's time that you sat your ass down and read his letter."

Lava turned to walk to the desk to retrieve the envelope.

Mr. Lamour chimed in.

"I'm in pain over here watching my two kids fight."

He pretended to have a heart attack, and then motioned to the security guards.

"Look at this. I trained these two. He's my Super Alpha Male that hates gays, by the way, I didn't know that. And look at her, if she had balls, she'd have to have an office with a window that opened, just so she could hang her nuts."

The two security guards pretended to laugh.

"Come over here and have a seat. This letter is nuclear kid. I have to do this to you, and I have never said this before to anyone. I actually don't want to do this. You're a good kid and you don't deserve this, but you do. It's called politics. Anyone can execute, but you have to know how to play this part of the game. And you have to know how to play it with everyone and every persuasion. Now our Mayor is gay. And she just so happens to be the wife of the President of the Board of Directors at Wellington and Wellington."

He threw his hands in the air and shook his head.

"Call it scapegoat, call it barbecue goat, you're fucking with my money."

"But it wasn't like that. I don't have a problem with anyone; regardless of their sexual preference. It's their choice and I respect other people's choices the way that I want them to respect mine."

He looked around the room as if to get the attention of people who were already giving him their attention. Satisfied that he owned the stage, Lamour continued.

"A White guy and a Black guy are thirsty. Each one gets up from their desk to go drink from the office water fountain located in the hall. The Black guy reaches the water fountain first and begins drinking. He's satisfied and he leaves to go back to his desk. All of a sudden the White guy stops dead in his tracks and returns to his desk. Another Black guy observes what takes place as he is exiting the bathroom and he too is thirsty and was walking to the water fountain behind the White guy without his knowing. He continues to the water fountain. Drinks until he is satisfied and then heads to the desk of the White guy. Upon arriving he looks in, taps on the desk lightly and says, 'You do know that it's okay to drink behind us Blacks. The worse that can happen is that you turn Black.' He starts laughing and the White guy jumps up and screams 'Hey I'm not RACIST!' But the truth is that he is. And he is so intrinsically racist that in his mind, if he doesn't drink from the water fountain before anyone Black, he would rather remain thirsty. What's that beautiful word we have to use now?"

Lava added, "Cognitive dissonance or implicit bias, take your choice. We all have the propensity to be racist and not know it."

Mr. Lamour and I both sat across from each other, with the security guards positioned behind me.

"Listen to me," Lamour said. You're saying that you're not homophobic. Wait. Wait. Wait. Actually," he looked at the Human Resource Director and then back at me. "You're ACTUALLY crying *'but it wasn't'* and *'but it wasn't.'* You sound like the white guy screaming I'm not racist. It's perception, and perception is truth. Perception is fact to the people that own it. Now shut the fuck up and read the letter. And before you do, I highly suggest you drink that delicious Scotch I gave you before that cube of ice ruins the elegance and flavor."

I swallowed all of it in one gulp and began to read.

20

....

AFTER MY TERMINATION and discussion of benefits, I ended up at Black People Park – a nickname Black people use, in our opposition to the park's true title–to sit and people watch. Many years ago, a rich, white guy bought out the land from up under the prior owners of the upscale Black suburb, evicted the owners, then flattened the homes and erected numerous statues of him throughout the park.

To the melanated culture, the park represents a time when Blacks lived to their utmost potential. They owned their own businesses, their own land, and their own banks, during a time when they were forced to live amongst themselves. Education was a priority and Black men wore suits.

However, overnight they were murdered, businesses burned and chased out of their homes. Then the white majority divided the deeds to their homes amongst themselves. Divided their land amongst themselves, and then birthed white children that pointed fingers at the melanated culture and asked, *'why don't they do better?'*

But we remember what the park was, how we were and what we can become. So we call it what we want regardless of the title given to it; we refuse to forget.

I sat and observed. I was exhausted. Way too many emotions in a forty-eight hour time span. My cell phone vibrated and buzzed me back to the present.

I was shocked that she called so soon. I thought maybe a week would past before I would hear from her, or simply never hear from her at all.

"Hello Lovely Lava."

"Are you surprised so soon? Don't answer that because I don't want you to lie to me again."

I smiled.

"Sorry, not sorry about today," she confessed. That's the problem with sleeping with someone in your chain of command. At some point, an opportunity presents itself where we are opponents in the ring. And all you can think about is not thinking about how good the sex is. Just throw punches and try not to look fake when you fall, right?"

"That's your interpretation of today's events?" I asked. "You were throwing punches, trying not to look fake, and at the same time thinking about how good the sex is?"

"About the sex; you don't work here anymore, but that was a convenience that I needed. This is a ridiculously stressful occupation," Lava responded then giggled.

"It's a convenience that you can keep. There are multitudes of hotels downtown. I can get one and text you the room number whenever you want."

"My husband knows damn near everyone in this city, and together we own at least a tenth of it. Even the building you live in, he owns ten floors through an LLC with some guys from college. The last thing I need is to be seen walking in any building owned by him and his partners. Oh shit! Two of them live there. I just thought about that, no fucking way!"

"So who's going to be the new and lucky guy to fulfill your office habits?"

I tried to sound unbothered.

"Don't know, any recommendations?" she giggled. "You know everything about everyone here; at least from a profile perspective."

Chapter Twenty

"No recommendations on giving another man the pleasure of taking my place. It took me some time to get over the awareness that I was sharing you with your husband," I said that with more emotion than I intended.

"Actually he was sharing me with you, and I cannot risk being seen outside of this building; unless it's directly to a function to stand by his side for support or straight home."

"I never knew he was so notorious. All this time I was nutting on you, and he was nutting on the city. He must really have a big dick because that's a lot of cum."

"It's half the size of yours. It feels great after a bottle of wine and masturbating in the bathroom while he's sleep, but his bank account would make you cry and question your value." I made note that she defended her man.

"Nothing could make me question my value." *For a moment I thought that my parents could*, "And for the record, I may have made a mistake, but I'm not homophobic."

"Now you say it." There was a long pause before Lava continued. "Mistakes happen, but I am going to miss you."

"Me or my penis?"

"Actually, your penis because I never really liked you. But since your OLD boss thinks I have an inner-Alpha male, I may just play with my own dick and hang my nuts out the window."

She laughed.

"He's such an ass, isn't he?"

"I'm going to miss you too." I finally spoke after another awkward pause between us. "I never met a woman so smart and freaky. You were the perfect R. Kelly song."

She laughed much harder than before.

"You always say the dumbest shit to be so smart. No one ever makes me laugh like you and I hate you for that."

She took a loud, deep breath into the phone.

"My husband stopped making me laugh years ago."

"No hard feelings. And you looked beautiful throwing punches by the way."

"I actually held back; those were my soft blows."

I could feel her smiling and wanted to hold on to that memory. I could suddenly taste her perfume. I didn't want to say good bye, but I didn't know what else to say. So I just hung up.

21

I DECIDED TO chill at Bowden Ballers due to it being Wednesday night. I was hoping Wounded Society would be available and charitable enough to donate some time to me. For once on this day, I actually got what I asked for.

Of course I had to wait, but that was cool. It gave me time to put something on my stomach and knock down two drinks before he sat down. Like a school girl, I had tears in my eyes as I replayed Greek's suicide, my word play with his wife, Petra, and then my love-hate exchange with Lava at the office while she fired me.

Wounded Society sat pensive, as if searching for the right questions, or maybe the right words. He stood up suddenly and moved his chair directly in front of mine, and then just over a whisper, Wounded Society began an extemporaneous poem;

"Oh how I love thee, Ms. Vagina so wet
Oh how I hate thee, making me your office pet
I knew you were married, but that ass made me weak
Now I feel anger, every time I hear you speak
You told me about your husband, and I stood and said 'SO'!
Now I'm wishing to turn back the hands of time,
To when we met, so I could say 'NO'!"

Wounded Society stood with one hand on his stomach, and the

other hand fisted in front of his mouth while he laughed. He patted his stomach with his right hand, and then began wiping his clothes with both hands as if he spilled an invisible drink.

"Give me a napkin Bro, I need to write that shit down."

He laughed and shook his head again. He emptied the glass holding the brown liquor and slammed it on the table.

"DAMN, you're having a bad week." He stroked his beard and looked around the bar. "I don't even know where to start."

Wounded shrugged dramatically, and turned from side to side.

"You got suicide. A man's wife blaming you for her husband cheating. A married woman sucking your dick on the job, who you made the mistake of falling in love with, only for her to ultimately respond by finding a way to fire you. And in my opinion, she played you to get rid of you. And let's not forget, you're also fucking your neighbor that literally lives across the hall from you. I feel like I need to get drunk just because you told me some shit I might not be able to forget in the morning. Bro, let's talk about white people, that's easier."

He leaned back in his chair and looked at me with eyes as wide as he could open them.

I laughed and it actually felt good.

"You think I'm an idiot for sleeping with these married women?"

"No sir! No sir! That pink stink does something strange to a man's mind, no matter the idiot and no matter the genius. I don't think you did anything wrong by tasting the pink stink. I think the problem is, 'Why did you *keep* tasting it?' Some pink you're just supposed to sample and put back where you found it; especially when somebody else owns it. It was never yours to keep. And telling her you love her was not smart."

He shook his head from side-to-side.

"Hopefully she let that shit go into the *'fictitious file.'* If not, she might pop up on your ass with some *'real life'* expectations."

"Come on Wounded, can a man ever own a woman's pussy? Married or not married, the woman is the She God, and gods don't worry about mortals. I believe that it's a huge mistake that men make. I had an episode at FAMU where I got it in my head that the pussy was mine. That girl taught me in the worse way to never make that mistake again. And women are right, WE DON'T OWN THEM OR THEIR PUSSY AND WE NEVER DID PERIOD! You have to let a woman be a woman, and use her pussy as she chooses. My Boss made a decision to bless me with her essence of mouth and or vagina when she chose. Remember, SHE CHOSE ME!"

"And look what being chosen got you?"

"So, basically, you're saying that I fired myself."

I closed my eyes and took a deep breath.

"It might be a good time to change plantations. I got too many memories in that office anyway."

"Plantation? Nah Bro, this is your moment to escape to freedom. You got the knowledge."

"And I will get the money from where? Blacks built this country. Blacks enriched this country. And what the white folk do? Steal our money, close our banks down, and then make us beg them to loan us our money that they stole. So, to leave the plantation owner you have to go beg a plantation owner; even self-employed. But it is something to think about."

"Stop making excuses and start using all of the knowledge, Knowledge. And don't worry about leaving the club tonight."

"What do you mean?" My face was now contorted into a ball of confusion.

"We bout' to empty us a bottle of something! You know I got a room in the back."

"I'm not touching the super sticky mattress. I live right across the street. We are good on that one. But we will finish a bottle, tho!"

My tensed body began to relax as I allowed all of my frustrations to fade away, if only for one night.

22

AN HOUR BEFORE the sun rise I walked out of Bowden Ballers and went home. I took a long shower and tried not to replay the events of the week.

Lava, Greek and the Gay Guy's faces seemed to take turns running through my mind, appearing in between thoughts, continuously disrupting my peace. I didn't feel bad for being fired, I felt confused. The same lack of empathy for others that got me on the plantation, became the same reason that got me kicked off the plantation.

Ain't that a bitch!

I got out of the shower and put on my bathrobe with the hoodie. I went to the kitchen to prepare a kettle of water for my tea. I looked over a pile of mail on a table when my doorbell rang. I knew who it was.

I answered the door, "Hey neighbor."

She walked in wearing actual clothes.

"I thought that I heard music and assumed you were home early."

She noticed the tea pot and shooed me away from the kitchen. I assumed a position on the second stool from the corner of the island and placed my feet on the first stool. After watching her get a clean cup for me, and retrieve a spoon and tea bag, she gave me her undivided attention.

"What's up?"

"I got fired yesterday but it's a really cool story. Do you have time?"

"Of course. When don't I have time? I never know when my husband's coming home, but apparently there's a rule that I didn't know about that says it can't be prior to midnight."

She pretended to check her watch and shrugged her shoulders theatrically. She took off her jacket and sat on my sofa.

"THE GAY GUY! And I'm not being an asshole; he actually used to introduce himself as 'THE GAY GUY' anyway, he was sent to me to be terminated. Over the course of our discussion, he says to me.... 'Oh pooh, my husband's going to kill me.' Call me an idiot but I didn't take his statement serious enough to log it or notify the authorities, and apparently his husband actually killed him.

"Now before you say anything. Technically I wasn't fired because I didn't follow procedure. Meaning, if you terminate a woman and she says, 'my husband's going to kill me;' serious or joking, we have to log it and notify the authorities.

"Now back to me. Had his husband just killed him and no one knew why, then that would have been fine. However, THE GAY GUY wrote a damn letter and sent copies to my office and an extremely notorious gay association. In which he implicated me specifically as being the catalyst to his impending death. And because of those letters, my boss, due to political pressures outside of his control, felt obligated to terminate me because I didn't do anything to protect THE GAY GUY."

"I'm sorry but what's his real name?"

"FUCK HIS REAL NAME! What's your real name? I've been fucking you for months and you haven't volunteered that information. I think that's strange and yet intentional. Or maybe I'm strange because I actually liked it. However, since I may be hanging around a little more than usual, it would be nice to know who the white girl is that blows me in the morning?"

She doesn't answer right away; just stares at me instead. I counted the seconds as I questioned the pigmentation of her white skin. During slavery, white men often slept with their Black inventory more than their own white wives. It was imperative to a slave master's legacy to impregnate every Black woman that he owned. Even when his white wife delivered him a child, he demanded their white baby enjoy the succulent milk of Black breast. As the white child grew, he or she ate daily food prepared by Black hands; food of an African culture.

And who knows how many white women birthed Black babies. They too enjoyed the Black stock. But since white men write our history books, that is a chapter they have decided to vacate. White and Black DNAs are so intertwined; every American really should be considered Black.

I accused her once of using a tan spray, but she demanded her skin color was natural. I smiled at the thought of white people actually being Black people. They can deny Black history. They can even lie about the white history they propagandize. But they cannot lie about the Black blood within them.

"When you found out he was killed did you feel remorse?" She asked me.

"Remorse would not be the correct superlative that I would use to describe my feelings *Becky*."

She smiled and shook her head at the name that I threw at her.

"I mean, I'm not the one who killed him, *Samantha*."

She giggled and shook her head again.

"A man was killed and that is awful. But *Victoria* baby, if it was as serious as he stated, he knew the crazy he was married to. Why didn't he do more to protect himself? Why did he even go home, *Jennifer*?"

She's laughed out loud and hid her face behind a couch pillow.

"Are these supposed to be *'white girl names'* because you are so far off?"

She waved an index finger from side-to-side at me.

"Ok, a few questions. During your termination, at any point, did you look at the person firing you and say that you were sorry? Or, did you shed a tear for this guy? Or, did you display any emotion at all that said you took full responsibility, and you wished this never happened?"

I yelled, "HELL NO I DIDN'T! I'm not going to allow someone... anyone to place a death on my shoulders. His husband killed him, not me. And it doesn't matter to me that he was gay, or a midget or a humpback whale. He was sent to my office to be terminated. The result when he got home would have been the same had it been anyone else that fired him. Don't you understand, *Pam*. I was fired because of the letter naming my company, naming me and others being notified, and now my company needs a scapegoat. I'm the goat not the murderer, *Karen*."

"It bothers me to know that a man would walk around the office calling himself the *Gay Guy*. Why do you think he did that?"

She had a sincere look on her face as she analyzed her own question.

I began to see his face again. I closed my eyes and shook my head.

"He was very flamboyant. I don't think he cared what people thought, and I don't think he felt it was important to hide his sexual preference. I actually think he relished in the attention. I'm sure there are many more homosexuals in that building, but they have aspirations and keep their sexual activities private. You'll never become the CEO running around calling yourself the *Gay Guy*; so there's a lack of maturity aspect to this as well."

She just sat there, staring at me. I didn't understand it.

"Judgment. Sex. Pity. Don't be so quiet, *Megan*. It's okay, and I'll be okay. I'm running out of white girl names by the way. You can interrupt me at any time, *Anne*."

"Don't you think it would ruin some of the excitement if you knew my name?" She gave me with a clever grin.

"I always wondered, do married women cheat because their bored? Is that what this is about, you're lacking excitement from your hubby? Has the honeymoon fire flamed out? Or, do you just get excited sexing Black men because it makes daddy angry?"

"Lack of excitement with my hubby is not what this is about. You have a gay guy story and I have a gay guy story."

She folded her arms and looked toward the window.

"I don't want to believe my husband is gay but there are some signs that make me wonder. You don't believe everything I say, and I can understand that. I mean, if what I say is true, why am I still with him, right?"

She never looked at me. And she was right. I never believed what married women told me. Had I believed, my brain would turn into a scrambled egg.

"So, is your husband the gay guy in this story, or is there another gay guy in this story? I just want to make sure that I know how many gay guys are in this story?"

I laughed but stopped once I realized she was serious.

She closed her eyes and looked like she was in physical pain, like she might vomit. She was clearly reliving some event that she had not shared with me. She jumped off the couch.

"A drink first please."

I watched her enter the kitchen, and then I closed my eyes and heard my boss's voice..."*gays are taking over.*"

I took a series of deep breaths and tried to clear my mind. I didn't want to think about anything. Not today. Not tomorrow. I just wanted a clear head. I felt a rush of sleepiness and jumped at her rubbing my neck. She handed me a drink and sat next to me. I noticed her hands were empty.

"Where's your drink?"

"Oh, I did like three shots in the kitchen."

She patted one of my legs and clapped her hands loudly. I downed my tequila and handed her the empty glass. She played with it and held her gaze somewhere across the room as she spoke.

"I know that you asked me not to talk about my husband during our initial..... um...what shall we call this?"

She turned her head sideways and focused on me.

"Neighborly...... fuck buddies?"

I interrupted her.

"I never borrowed sugar, and it's called *human*. We have needs. Primal needs. Your lion is not serving his queen. So, you roamed the jungle and found another lion. It's just human nature *Judy*. Don't make being human menacing."

"I'm cheating on my fucking husband, and that's natural?"

"Of course! And nothing else. Because if you categorize it as something else, you demean US! Our character, as if we are not a part of the human species. Cheating is human. It's natural, so natural that it's not even cheating. It's a basic human function. Hell, it was your European ancestors that invented monogamy. We didn't have that shit in Africa."

She didn't laugh.

"I guess we both have to justify what we do. But anyway."

She dropped her head and began spinning the glass in her hands again.

"I feel like I never know when my husband is coming home. He always says the same thing. *'I'm learning this market. I'm in the car with Trevor and I don't want him in our conversations. I'm with a client and can't talk.'* It's always Trevor. *'Trevor told me to. I'm busy with Trevor. I need this job and don't want to upset Trevor. Trevor is my Supervisor, and he monitors and grades everything. Trevor, Trevor, Trevor and more Trevor.'* We haven't had sex in about six months."

She pointed a finger in my direction without making eye contact.

"Maybe this is why I chose you? My hormones were everywhere and I was really confused as to why I was lonely. It just seemed sudden. We went from newlyweds to roommates to me being alone most of the time. I didn't get married to be by myself. Not like this. Anyway, I'm trying to give you the short version. One night he comes home a little after one in the morning, and plops down on his back on the couch, and completely passed out. I had been waiting all day to take him. No matter what he said. I was going to take the dick. No questions and no excuses about work or Trevor were going to stop me. I come out of the bedroom and I hear him breathing heavy and I think to myself, this asshole is completely faking sleep. I know how he sounds when he's asleep."

"I'm completely naked wearing red lipstick and red high heels. I go over to the couch and undo his belt."

She set down the glass and started to move her hands, reenacting the actual scene.

"I undo his pants. Pull the zipper down and pull his pants and underwear down and I...."

She covered her mouth and rocked back and forth, but I don't think she realized that her rocking picked up speed. She jumped off the couch and began walking around the coffee table. She circled the coffee table twice, and then sat on top of it, directly in front of me. She stared at her feet.

"I know this is going to sound looney but hear me out. I wanted a reaction. I wanted something from my husband of emotional value. So, I had an idea. I ran back in the room to go get my dildo. In my head I would pull his pants and underwear down, and act like," she made finger quotes, "I was going to stick it in his ass. He would jump up yelling and screaming. We would have this big, ugly, emotional argument where everything that I wanted to say comes out. He would yell back at me and then we would have the greatest fucking make up sex in the history of fucking make up sex, and then we would start acting like a married couple again. No more Trevor and no more you. We get back to us."

After several deep breaths, she noticed the empty glass on the floor. She picked it up and closed her eyes.

"But in reality, after I pulled his pants and underwear down, I acted like I'm pushing the dildo in, but it slid right in."

She looked at me wide eyed.

"It was like his ass was already lubricated. I didn't even have to push it in. His ass just fucking swallowed it and he didn't even budge. He just kinda said ....ooooooo! And then he did this girly giggle that I never heard come out of his mouth before and rolled over on his stomach. So, now I'm standing up looking down at my husband with the full length of a dildo up his ass and he doesn't SCREAM!

A few days later I decided that I would force him to bring Trevor to the house for dinner, or we meet somewhere for dinner. But I demanded that I meet Trevor, the man who had so much control over my husband. And then the day came."

She placed her hands on her face and began rubbing up and down. Then she began rubbing her knees and asked me, "the Gay Guy's name please?"

I yielded, "Keon Patience."

"Had he not told you he was gay, would you have known?"

"As soon as he opened his mouth, Stevie Wonder would have known. He's the utterly flamboyant type."

"I tried to have a clear mind and not judge. But we decided that I would meet them at a restaurant. Since their office is closer to downtown, it wouldn't make sense to come back to get me. However, I called my mom and told her what happened. I didn't want to but I needed to talk to someone. My mom told me to show up to the restaurant early, and sit somewhere where I would see them, but they wouldn't see me and monitor their interaction. Were they touchy feely? Did they act like lovers? So, I took her advice and got there really early and waited."

She took another deep breath.

"I fucking knew immediately, from the moment I saw them approaching the restaurant from outside that they had a relationship beyond work. There was a playful giddiness about them, like lovers who wanted to rip each other's clothes off, but they're in public and are trying to behave. But you could just tell by the closeness of their walk."

She closed her eyes again.

"I may have seen them holding hands, but I think they let go as they were crossing the street. When I approached the table, my husband was odd and Trevor NEVER EVER greeted me. He never LOOKED at me. He stared at Elijah the entire time. Never once did he look in my direction or acknowledge me. Every time I asked a question, the two of them just giggled and kept looking at each other. Like they had an inside joke but didn't want to share it with me."

"So finally, I had enough and I asked, *'What is going on? Can one of you just tell me?'* And that's when Trevor stood up and said *'I can't do this'* and walked out. Elijah looked confused. He rose to chase Trevor then sat back down. Then he turned and stared at the door and then turned around. He looked pained and I felt stupid and ridiculous. But I knew the answer to my question without them saying anything. Their actions practically yelled at me."

I raised my hand like I did back in high school, and she nodded.

"I am so sorry, but you left me hanging with the dildo up his ass on the couch. How in the hell did that night end? Did he jump up fussing and cussing? Did he nut all over the couch? What the hell happened?"

"I went back to my room and got in the bed. I just laid there. Staring at the ceiling trying to figure out how did I get here? How did we get here? Were there signs that I should have seen? Is he gay? Is he bisexual? How far am I willing to go to save my marriage? When morning came, I heard him moving around and eventually, he popped his head in the room and said *'BEST SLEEP EVER, can you wash that for me? I left it in the sink. Bye hun.'* Then he left for work. When I got up later the dildo was in the bathroom sink."

"He left the dildo in the sink and asked you to wash it?"

"Yep!"

"And then left for work?"

"Yep!"

I got up to get another drink.

"And you're trying to figure out if this dude is GAY? That is CRAZY as hell. I don't believe in hitting women but you try to stick anything other than your tongue in my ass, I'mma show you my best impersonation of Ike Turner."

I walked to the kitchen and continued talking at the same time. I made a drink, came back and laughed.

She was catatonic; a white mannequin on a Black man's coffee table. Her eyes were open but she wasn't blinking. I only read about this but never saw it up close. The rigidity of her posture held an air of death. I waved my hands in front of her face several times but didn't touch her.

I glanced at my walls of books and thought about American history. Just twenty years before I was born, Black children, such as Emmitt Till, were killed for looking at white women. Today they pass their pussy around to Black men like skittles; who wants some? Never giving thought or deference to the wishes of their great, great, great grandfathers of the lynching kind; the admirers and collectors of 'strange fruit.'

I don't believe in God. But if she does exist, and it would have to be a she because only women command such powers as both, creating men through birth and destroying men through words. Only women get to decide whether or not we have sex or we just talk. Only women get to decide that it was him who put something in my drink forty years ago, so lock him up today. And even if it wasn't him, and even if I may be wrong, or I may be making this up, still lock him up because he resembles the man in my imagination, and that man was *Black*. And no I didn't say anything forty years ago, but I'm a woman and I'm speaking today; and today I want what I want because I'm God.

And I don't believe in heaven, a place with no pain is a place for no life. For life without pain is a life without women. Who better causes pain than a woman that you can't have, or a woman that you want but doesn't want you? Or a woman you want but is already taken and only gives what she wants you to have because she's married; more power to the 'She God.' I sit and look at this woman, never knowing when she is lying or when she is telling the truth, but knowing that she could tell me and her husband whatever she feels in the moment. Giving both of us just enough information to keep us apart, or bring us together in a violent collision. Him fighting for a sanctimonious vow to protect his wife, and me fighting because I believed her words to be sanctimonious and our sex biblical.

Since I don't believe in God, and since I don't believe in heaven, I have to wonder if I'm wrong and they both exist. Did the She God allow Emmett Till some white pussy in that place called heaven? She had to have seen what took place to lead him to stand in front of her. Or did she turn all Black men into *Emmetts,* and say have fun in his honor? For now, skittles are yours to enjoy at will.

American history is amazing. Almost comical except the Black people keep dying at the end of every story. Or robbed. Or mis-educated. Or lynched. Or set on fire. Or dismembered. Or not allowed to vote. Or simply drugged with medication and sometimes drug behind trucks with confederate flags.

Or my very favorite part of American history, the story ending with Blacks on their knees begging for white approval. Beg while singing. Beg while dancing. Beg while praying but always begging for white affirmation. There is no gangster movie more gangsta than American history; it's my favorite channel.

23

SHE STARTED COUGHING and gasping for air. I had grabbed W.E.B Du Bois' *The Souls of Black Folk* from a shelf, and read a little bit while waiting for her to return from a moment in time that held her prisoner. I placed the book back on the shelf and brought her a glass of water.

She was still coughing when I sat the water in front of her. After gulping the water like a fish out of water returning to its habitat, she stood and began walking around my apartment, shaking her arms and legs to stimulate the circulation of blood flow.

Without looking at me or even in my direction, she said, "My name is Keisha by the way."

"NO WAY! I knew your ass was BLACK! No white woman names her daughter Keisha. I mean if you study the history of this country, then you know that *'everyone is Black,'* but your skin tone and your name is Keisha. You're killing me here. Someone in your family really liked the slaves."

She was doing squats in between leaning against the wall and pulling her ankles to the back of her buttocks. Holding to the count of ten and then squat and switching to the other ankle. After four repetitions she looked quizzically at me.

"Were we talking about something? Or did I fall asleep on you?"

I had to think about this question. Was this a game? Was this real? Was anything she saying real or was she the female 'Kizer Sosay;' taking ingredients from my gay guy story and reshuffling to deliver a gay guy story even bigger and better than mine back to me?

Would she suddenly rise and dramatically limp pathetically out of my condo smirking, only to straighten her legs after ten paces to an easy, cool stride while bathing in the enjoyment of knowing that I was fooled. Having me forever thinking her husband walked around with a shitty dick while acquiescing to the demands of an imaginary Trevor.

Nah, I was good. She could reverse ninja my shit and I wasn't even going to be mad. She doesn't need to finish a story that I wouldn't believe anyway. Married women cheat because married women are the ultimate She Gods. And She Gods don't need stories or excuses when they have wet vaginas.

I snapped back to reality.

"No Keisha Boo, you simply fell asleep baby. It must have been the shots you took. I think you drank them way too fast."

I faked a smile. Then I faked a laugh. She still stood, hands on her hips, head tilted back with her eyes closed; she still stretched but I wouldn't let her stretch my mind.

"FUCK! I zone out when I'm stressed. Or confused. I need to leave. Her eyes popped open and her head bobbed side-to-side. I'm going to see my mother and I'm not sure if I'm coming back. Something is going on with my husband. I didn't sign up for this, and I don't want to get stuck wasting time waiting on him to decide what he wants. Me or Trevor."

"So, you're just going to skip over the Black name like you didn't hear me?"

"A lot of Black women have this name but no name is owned by a color. There are white Keishas too."

"Wow, so says the power of white privilege. You can jack anybody shit and it just is. But Blacks intentionally choose specific white names in hopes of being accepted or treated better. To get in the good, white school, or to get that good, corporate job. You're white with a Black name, and you would still get the better job and everything else y'all are privileged to."

"So, you're just going to skip over the fact that I just told you that I'm leaving. I-MAY-NOT-COME-BACK! Can you comment on that without any references to American history, Black or white please Malcolm X?"

I threw my hands in the air and then plopped down on the couch.

"This relationship was going to end at some point anyway. It's not like I asked you to leave your husband, or like you even loved me. And if you did, you never told me."

She held that stare again; the one that I couldn't read. We were two people in the same room with no words, staring at each other. Until she broke the silence.

"I want to have sex with you before I leave please. Just sex."

She began taking off her clothes.

That 'She God' was a mean bitch, always throwing her pussy around to get what she wants. I watched her undress and came to a realization that made me sad. I was about to lose my second relationship with a married woman, in the span of one week.

What was I scared of? The fear of being normal. Normal men had one woman that wasn't married. Normal men dated until they found 'the one' and got married. I didn't want to be normal.

And I don't want to get married. Marriage drove my mother to an early death and my father crazy. Marriage led to Greek jumping off a bridge to kill himself, and Petra bitter. I'll take anything but marriage.

She walked over to stand in front of me as I was still sitting.

First, she locked her legs and bent over to bite my left ear lobe as she untied my robe.

Then, fully naked, she placed her hands on my shoulders, straddled me and threw her head back. I call it the white girl move. Her hair levitated in slow motion, to the side and down her back, exposing her neckline.

I was erect instantly. It wasn't the whiteness of her skin that drove me crazy. It was the freedom she gave me with her body. She allowed me to do anything. Any position. Anywhere in my apartment. The word no evaporated from her internal, vernacular dictionary. No matter how many times I would get erect, she would always be wet and ready.

If this really was going to be the last time, I wanted to do something that I hadn't done before. I picked her up, allowed my robe to fall onto the living room floor and then waved my finger side-to-side and whispered "not yet."

Her body trembled with anticipation and her eyes kept going up and down, begging for my hardness, yet watching my eyes for instructions and permission to do whatever I tell her. After walking backwards several steps I said, "Get on your hands and knees and crawl to me."

She dropped down immediately, palms down to the floor, head back, mouth open with her legs bent, ankles at her buttocks. If I had a camera it would have made one helluva picture. She had to have seen that pose somewhere.

She witnessed the excitement in my eyes and asked me, "Do you like this?"

In an effort to regain control, I put one finger to my mouth for her to be quiet and then, using the same finger, motioned her to crawl forward. It was then that she actually raised her hands and knees and began moving toward me. Just when she was inches from putting me in her mouth, I began moving backwards again, until my back was against the shared wall with the exterior hall; the hall that led to her apartment.

Unbeknownst to either of us, on the other side of the wall, Elijah left the elevator and contemplated how to confront his wife; for better or for worse.

As he walked down the hall and got closer to his and his neighbor's doors, he heard loud, muffled, sexual moans. As Elijah pulled out his key, the moaning caused him to reflect on the fact that he had sexually and emotionally neglected his wife.

When she got close enough again, I allowed her to insert the head of my penis into her mouth. I wanted to say that she couldn't leave. I wanted to say come back and see me. But it would have been the sex talking.

I had to stop myself from speaking. I bit my tongue. I bit my lips. We breathed harder and harder with our feelings amplified from the intimacy.

I couldn't take it anymore. I grabbed her to lift her off the floor. I turned her around, threw her against the wall, and raised her vagina to my mouth. My left arm was extended, while my left hand grabbed her neck. I placed her legs on my shoulders, while my right hand gripped her left thigh. Her hands grabbed my head, and she arched her back repeatedly riding my tongue.

She yelled in ecstasy.

Elijah heard a muffled yell, pulled his key out of his front door, and decided to go back downstairs. He would not disturb his wife or hurt her any more than he already had. What he had to say could wait. He would hurt her some other day.

He shuffled back to the elevator, and tried not to think about the sounds from behind the neighbor's walls; the hard bangs, muffled moans, and frequent gasp of heavy breathing. When the elevator door closed he felt panicked. Breaking up would never be easy, and now he had to prepare himself for another fight; a routine quarrel with his lover that was losing its sustainability. Elijah exited the building and got back in the car.

"That was quick," Trevor said. "How did she take it? Darling, what did she say? Was she even home?"

Elijah ignored Trevor and adjusted his seat to buy time. Then he adjusted the rearview mirror.

"The seat is fine and the mirror is fine. I'M NOT FINE! Can you answer my fucking questions PLEASE!" Trevor yelled, irritated.

Elijah leaned back in his seat, started the car, and then looked at Trevor. The car didn't move and his mouth wouldn't move. Then he rose forward, grabbed the steering wheel with both hands, and banged his head softly and repeatedly against it. He refused to look at Trevor as he spoke.

"I froze again. I'm sorry but I froze again."

He jumped back into the cushioning of his seat and raised his hands in the air.

"I heard my neighbor wall banging some chick, and it made me realize that much more how much I've neglected JoHannah."

"So what does that mean?" Trevor took a deep breath and clutched at his heart. "Do you need to fuck her to get the strength and courage you need to tell her that you're gay? That you never liked women. Do you need to give her some ATTENTION before informing her that none of this is real? That you don't have a job. That you leave the house in the morning to go be with the man that you should have married. That said man is the one that has been paying your fucking rent, utilities and putting food in the fucking refrigerator to help keep up a ruse because you're too chicken shit to just be you. And being you means being with me. You FREEZE every time, give me some bullshit excuse, and now I'm tired. I'm just tired. When is this going to end? I need an answer Elijah."

Elijah drove the car down the street in silence. The heat from Trevor's stare could have melted the side of his face. After two rights and a left, he pulled over into a parking spot and placed the car in park. He turned to face the pain in Trevor's eyes.

"JoHannah did something that I haven't told you."

He hesitated then laughed hysterically.

Trevor had more than lost his patience, he felt betrayed. He moved his head from side-to-side, and allowed the tears to flow from his eyes.

He looked into his window and spoke to his reflection, "It's always going to be like this."

He sniffled and screamed.

"WHAT THE FUCK IS SO FUNNY? STOP FUCKING LAUGHING!"

Elijah spoke in between laughs.

"I left your place later than I should have. When I got home, I didn't undress and just plopped down on the couch. I fell asleep instantly, so I don't know when she did it. BUT! She put a fucking dildo up my ass and left it there. I swear to you."

Chapter Twenty-Three

Trevor shook like a wet dog.

"Well that doesn't make any sense. Why the fuck would she do that? Wait! WHO DOES THAT?"

They both stared at the other.

"What the fuck does that even mean, Elijah?"

"It means that it's over. A conversation will just make it official."

He took a deep breath, rubbed his stomach, and continued.

"Listen to me. It doesn't take a genius to figure that just maybe we had something going on after your dramatic scene at the restaurant. You might as well have come in with a sign that said, "Hey Johanna, I'm sucking and fucking your HUSBAND!"

Elijah pulled his shirt out of his pants and pulled it to his face to dry his eyes, cheeks and nose.

Snapped out of shock, Trevor grabbed Elijah's right arm.

"Dude this is so sick. I mean, you never know how someone's going to react when they find out you're gay, but she left a dildo in your ass while you were sleeping. Fuck! Ok, so there's some hope. Now when are you going to have this, official break up, conversation with your wife?"

Elijah took a deep breath.

"Saturday!"

Another deep breath.

"This Saturday!"

I continued to sex her like it really was going to be our last time. With every thrust I pounded my goodbyes, and with each release of wetness, she replied with gratitude. After it was over, we laid on the floor of the living room, panting. She asked me my name in between breaths. And in case she was lying about hers, I lied about mine too, and said it was Emmett.

"So when are you leaving me?"

"I'm not leaving you, I'm leaving my husband," she took a deep breath. "I have to figure out what to do with you. But I made arrangements to leave Saturday."

Another deep breath.

"I'm leaving him this Saturday."

24

AFTER KEISHA LEFT, I thought about every white woman I ever slept with. I thought about how easy it was for me to get them, and how skittles symbolized the white woman's vagina. After all, Black women gave up their cookies, so white women needed a pet name for their vagina too. I was stuck somewhere in between a dream and being awake; my body in a pool of sweat.

I was having an epiphany within a dream. My mind's own inception, declaring '*I know why George killed Trayvon.*'

One minute I was thinking and analyzing my relationship with white women, and the next minute I was preparing to spend eternity screaming at the top of my lungs as if George was right in front of me. As if American't was an actual person.

I couldn't help but think about Trayvon Martin. Although I had no children of my own, I saw him as a younger version of me. It grieved me that a child of my race could be viewed as a threat and not simply as a child.

It bothered me that I lived in a country that got angry at Black children because of the skin color they *chose*. It bothered me that I lived in a country that would rather see a child of my race dead instead of delivering joy with their laughter. I see Trayvon walking home and I question the state of mind that George possessed; a minority attacking a minority of a darker status.

Big Brains forced his way into my dream screaming vehemently..... ANOTHER FUCKING GEORGE!!! What did George see? How did George feel? As Trayvon walked in his blue jeans and hoodie, something everyone has worn at some point in their life, did George really feel disturbed or threatened? Could he not tell the difference between an adult and a child?

Was our skin color that deleterious that we ignited anger just by waking up, at any age, getting dressed, at any age, and walking outside, at any age? I yelled, "The white people won't accept you as one of them. That will never happen, George. You're Hispanic ass is a Nigger too. You're a Nigger too, George! You attacked the wrong person. He was not your enemy. Blacks and Hispanics share love and a common foe."

Trayvon was simply returning home while holding his favorite candy–skittles. The white emblem of the white vagina. However, Trayvon was too young to know such a thing. He probably was thinking about a video game, if anything, or maybe returning home to watch a movie.

The power of white psychological warfare has damaged everything that is not white. George is not white. Yet, the white voice in his head spoke and told him to protect something that will never be his to own; the white man's respect and the white man's pride and joy, his skittles. George chose to protect the skittles! And it was our Black responsibility to protect Trayvon. And in the absence of Black, it was his brown responsibility to protect our Black child.

Trayvon is dead. George is still alive, yes George is still alive. *I hear Big Brains again screaming vehemently.....ANOTHER FUCKING GEORGE!!!*

Yet, as I pondered this scenario of a free George and a dead Trayvon, I have realized that this episode is symbolic of something else. The *'invisible white knee'* that my race has always felt.

Trayvon is only one example of the knee that arrives on our neck at birth. I couldn't protect you Trayvon, and for that, on behalf of your father and me, we apologize. Trayvon is dead and George is free. The white man chose to protect George and reward him for *'his brave act of standing his ground against a child.'* But what he did was not right in our eyes. In our eyes he killed one of our babies. In our eyes he is a fucking coward that should spend the rest of his life behind bars, or an imaginary place called hell, where I heard *'bad people'* burn for eternity. I know hell is not real, but at times like this, it at least sounds good.

Religion sits somewhere between freedom and equality. Waking up Black and living in American't, I can attest to you that freedom and equality are illusions to my race. It's the white man's government that specializes in illusions. And it's the white man that gave us his religion, the most disgusting illusion of them all. A slave master and a slave cannot pray to the same god in no universe. I preserve the assessment that his beliefs are unsavory for my people. Because if religion was real, the white man would do everything that he could in his power, and with the weight of his government, to keep it a secret. The white man would deny us the possession of it. I cannot fathom a white man wanting to see my Black ass in heaven sitting next to him, when on earth, in this life, he cannot stand my Black presence in *'his country.'*

All good things are denied to Black people. Like protection. Protection is real. The white man gave Trayvon's family the illusion of religion, but then denied protection to the same family's child. If it would bring Trayvon back, I would give religion back. I would prefer my Black children to live in a country that protects and not prays. Trayvon is dead. George is free. And there was not one religion that could have saved Trayvon when he needed it most.

For this, I cannot fathom allowing a child of my seed to be born in this country. Because in this country, a child born of a slave will always be a slave, and I am not yet free. And I have to wonder if even Trayvon is. We apologize.

My cell phone rang and snatched me from mental purgatory. My cell phone rang and George disappeared. My cell phone rang and

Trayvon waved goodbye. My cell phone rang and I missed my skittles. My skittles were leaving Saturday. I tried to roll over but felt the weight of the world on my shoulders. I blinked several times, trying to escape purgatory and return to the salvation of my bed. My mind was foggy and my sheets were heavy from a working mind.

By the time I gained the strength and consciousness to answer the phone, it was too late.

Seconds later I got a voicemail notification. I tossed the phone and stared at my blue ceiling. I've painted every ceiling everywhere that I've ever lived blue; sky blue. I don't want anything white telling me how high I can rise. Racism is in everything. White people paint ceilings white to remind Blacks that they can go only as high as they want until they hit their heads; against the ceiling. So I figured, if the sky's the limit, let me remind myself. I will never possess a white ceiling, no matter how many times I trick a white woman into believing that she can possess me.

Goodbye Keisha or whatever your name is.

I reclaimed my deliverance and awoke with a need to see my father. Not that I thought anything bad had happened. I just wanted my Dad. He was on my mind as I rose from bed to hit the shower. We met every Tuesday before I went to work. And even though there's no work anymore, I looked at it as more time to spend with him, and plan my future.

My father and I meet in front of a *Chinese restaurant called Chi-Chi*. He took me there for years as I was growing up. The cool thing about the restaurant is that, not only did I grow up eating there, but one day on the campus of FAMU, I saw this Chinese kid sitting by himself on the set. I knew he looked familiar but couldn't figure out why. I walked over and introduced myself.

"Where do I know you from?"

"My family's restaurant. I cook in the back, and sometime I see you when I'm cleaning tables. We never officially met but my name is Lu Ling."

"I'm not trying to be funny, but what made you decide to attend school at a historically Black college."

"My dad is cheap! One day he looked at me and said, 'two plus two is the same there as two plus two at a more expensive and predominantly white school.' So why pay more, it's always going to be two plus two."

"Sounds like your father is a smart man."

And just like that we became friends. He went right back to his family restaurant after graduation, but this time as a manager.

Years later, I was at work and Lu Ling called me to say that there was a Black man with no legs sitting in front of the restaurant at the curb singing. He thought it might be my father and that I needed to come get him before his father did something crazy to make him leave.

Understandably, it could be bad for business. But almost two hours later, when I arrived, Lu's father was sitting next to mine, eating and caring on a conversation like the best of friends. Lu explained to his dad how friendly I was, and how I was the only person that approached him without judgment.

And that simple act of kindness throughout his time at FAMU made his experience all the better. After hearing his son's story, Lu's dad decided to reciprocate my act of kindness to my father. I gave Lu a crazy, big hug that day and he prepared us some lo mien, and then all four of us were sitting on the curb talking. It was one of the most humane moments of my life; an absolutely beautiful moment on a beautiful day.

When I got to the corner of Chi-Chi's that day, I didn't see my father. I walked into the restaurant and waited to be acknowledged by the hostess. I asked for Lu and she bowed politely and turned to retrieve him.

He came out from an office and gave me a big smile and then seemed hesitant with his words. "I hope that you don't get mad at me. But your dad came by and left you a letter about two days ago.

He asked me not to contact you, but wait until you showed up today to give it to you."

I thought about the last letter I received at my office. Hopefully this one would be a lot better. I took the letter and stared at my father's hand writing like it was hieroglyphics. It's one of those small details in life that you don't think about, your parent's handwriting.

I took a look at Lu and he seemed pained. I pulled him by the shoulder to me and embraced him.

"I'm not mad brother. You and your family have been nothing but respectful to me and my father. You are a loyalist. Loyal to all you love. I'm sure by him asking you to do this, you felt like you might be betraying me. But it's cool. To me, it shows that you got love for my father, just as much as for me, and you wanted to honor his request. If your father was still alive and asked me to help him with anything, and not tell you, I would have done it because I had a tremendous amount of respect for him as well. You and I are good Lu. Relax brother."

We dapped up, and I walked outside so no one would see the tears that formed in the corners of my eyes.

When my father's health began deteriorating, I thought living with me would help him. I wanted to provide him with a safe, clean environment, but it didn't help. He kept waking up screaming and would always refuse to cut off his bedroom light at night. There were times when I would walk in his room and he would be asleep on the floor in the bathroom instead of in his bed. And one day I woke up and he was gone. He came back two days later.

One day I woke up and he was gone again. He came back two weeks later.

One day I woke up, and he was gone again. But he never came back after that.

Then I got a call almost a year later that there had been an accident, and when I arrived at the hospital, he was lying there with no legs and a big smile. He just started talking like he didn't notice the difference. The hospital personnel didn't have an answer and he never gave them or me one.

I went back the next day to sit with him and they said that he left. A man with no legs checked himself out. Almost another year later was when I got the call from Lu that he was in front of the store singing.

I started walking, not even knowing where I was going. I just wanted to be moving and keep moving. Afraid to stop physically because then I would move mentally. And I wasn't sure that I could keep up with all of my thoughts.

Maybe that's how you lose your sanity.

You stop moving physically and your mind takes over. Jumbling everything together because you never really had anything together in the first place. You just kept physically moving and trying not to think about everything and focus on the one thing that you could control; nothing.

I stopped suddenly and looked into a store front window at my reflection. I had been avoiding my reflection, because to see one's reflection is to reflect.

Lava called me out on my bullshit. Petra called me out on my bullshit. And my best friend took memories and statements from my past, that only he knew, sharpened them into a spear, and stabbed my ass. Calling me out on my bullshit.

I don't remember moving my hands, but suddenly the envelope was open that my father left me. My heart raced. Breathing became difficult. I closed my eyes and pulled the letter up to read it.

I calmed myself with a breathing exercise.

I opened my eyes and saw three words my father had written; Nganga Nyjuan Nzumbi. My real name. I had forgotten my real name.

When I was eight years old, I got into my first fist fight with a boy in my neighborhood. I didn't know my father watched me get my ass kicked. When I came home crying, he was sitting on the couch with his arms folded. His face was stoic. No matter where or how animated I moved, only his eyes followed.

He asked me, "Why are you crying?"

Lying, as children do, I replied, "I was running and fell and it hurt."

My father told me to come closer, and once I was in arms reach, he punched me in the chest so fast, I never saw it coming. I screamed in the fetal position at the top of my lungs, when my mom ran into the living room.

She yelled at my father, but he never took his eyes off of me.

He simply told my mother, "This is between a father and his son. If I don't do this now, he'll get his ass whooped for the rest of his life."

Pissed but understanding the machismo of who was talking, she simply shook her head and abandoned me.

My father screamed at me, "SHUT UP AND STAND UP!"

I rose and looked into the eyes of the only man that struck fear into me to this day.

"I don't care about these little boys giving you a nickname. I don't even care about you giving people a nickname for yourself. But what I do care about is that you never forget your name, and what your name stands for. I named you after the first African to escape from his slave master and rise to royalty, and become a king. Your name means 'great lord, or protector of the community.' I named you after an African warrior, and to denounce the last name that this family inherited from the white people who once owned us. You'll be the beginning of an entirely new legacy."

He grabbed me with his hands and rose from the couch, lifting my small body off the floor and into the air in front of him.

"Whenever you need strength. Whenever you get confused. Whenever life kicks your butt and your feeling depressed, I want you to get off your ass, no matter where you are, stand up and say your name. Because if you stop saying your REAL NAME, that is when you will get lost."

I looked back at my reflection and spoke, "My name is Nganga Nyjuan Nzumbi." I forgot the meaning of my name.

25

I NOTICED HER first. I believed that everyone noticed her first. Petra always held a presence, as if her aura necessitated authority. She sat wide across the seat of two chairs. From my vantage point, her eyes were recalcitrant. She was not the type of woman to be defeated. Not even by the death of her husband.

Petra held her head high in a multicolored, silk wrap. She adorned a black dress that covered the entirety of her body. She didn't cry and did not seem to be in any pain. She possessed a look of expectation, as if she had dreamed this so many times, cried so many times, that now that it actually happened, her tear ducts were empty; never to cry for Greek again.

Her skin was a black hue of pure perfection. There were no scars, no wrinkles, or even a faint sign that her face or hands had ever been scratched; although, that was all she ever allowed the public to see. She was not Muslim; she was a woman of virtue. Seeing Petra and Greek holding hands for the first time, I couldn't help but look at her and think, 'how in the hell did he manage to convince this woman to be with him?'

The contrast was barefaced.

"DAMN PETRA," I uttered as I hid. Standing behind a tree, I turned my attention to Greek's children, four sat to Petra's left and three to her right. Even they possessed a look of obstinacy, and if their mother didn't cry, nor would they. She was their fearless leader, forever training them to be ladies.

A wind blew from behind me. It kidnapped the scent of my cologne and, laughingly delivered it to the crest of Petra's nostrils. Her face began to twist and her nose flared, her big chest quickly rose, and as she exhaled, collapsed slowly. Her head snapped left, scanned the audience, and then it snapped right, still scanning. It was then that I realized how hard she was trying to keep it together.

She closed her eyes and shook her head and then I felt a pain. I owed you an apology, Petra. She wanted a husband to give her commitment, integrity and loyalty, and Greek failed miserably. She wanted Black men to just meet her expectations of being men. And although I wasn't her husband, as a friend and godfather to her children, I also failed to meet her expectations. I owed you an apology, Petra.

She opened her eyes, and even though I thought that I was far enough away from the actual funeral to be noticed, I felt caged by her stare. Can I be seen? Did I make a mistake and disturb the sanctity of her grief? My cologne travelled and Petra realized that I defied her again. My presence affirmed that I was like Greek. I couldn't be trusted to do what she asked. I thought to myself, there's no way she can see me. But then I smiled. She was a Black woman, the most powerful species on the planet. They possessed so many superpowers, that if anyone at the funeral could see me, even moving back and forth from behind a tree, of course it would be Petra.

There was no way I was not coming to this funeral. What the hell was Greek thinking; leaving behind his wife and children like this. I couldn't hear what was being said, but I could see faces with tears, and drenched handkerchiefs. Everyone was crying except Petra and her children. As the pastor spoke, I saw heads nod in agreement.

I saw my FAMU brothers standing with their wives and children. They looked distinguished in a way that I have not considered or witnessed prior. I'm the only one single, and I just realized that no one would have been standing next to me, had I been allowed to attend. Such juxtaposition to our actual relationships. All of them surrounded and supported by love, and me with my thoughts. I pulled my cell phone out to send a text through our group chat. But thought better of the idea and decided to wait. This was Greek's moment, not mine.

Maybe it's because I can't hear anyone at the funeral that my mind began to wonder. I looked up at the clouds and saw a plane in the far distance, but there was no sound. I wished W.E.B. DuBois was our first, Black President of the United States. He never would've allowed drones to fly around other countries killing people that may or may not be the right targets. But it wasn't, we got Obama, and he did.

I wished Malcom X could've given us his version of the '*I have a Dream*' speech at the Washington Monument. I'm sure his speech would've been *WOKE*, and economically benefited Black people. But it wasn't, we got the guy who dreamed of us sharing a water fountain with white folk at a time when no one Black owned a water fountain; nonetheless, an actual building. So, we still had to walk into their building, and we still had to pay rent. And he dreamed a dream where we swallow our pride and turn the other cheek when the white man punches us, kicks us, or bombs our children. And now our children, being born of Black generations of men and women who swallowed their dignity, until their generation said '*fuck pulling up our pants*' because we don't have any pride and our cheeks hurt. So, we are going to smoke this weed to take away the pain of that entire inherited cheek turning bullshit.

I wished someone white got beat by nine, Black police officers and it was secretly recorded and exposed by the news media. But it wasn't. It was just another Black man, ironically with the last name *King*. And yes, there were protest, but nothing changed. We still wake up Black and they still beat us; and yet, we still protest. I wondered how many more protest we will have to have to be recognized as human in our own country.

Then we witnessed George Floyd's murder and I had an epiphany. There has always been a proverbial, white knee on the Black race. Never blatant and always subtle, but we felt it. And it hurt worst to actually see it; the deliberate comfort of a white man killing one of us with his knee. Void of emotion or displaying the same emotion as if taking out the trash. And maybe that's what the police officer thought he was doing.

Suicide is a romantic phenomenon, even considered a love song in certain Asian countries. It's your mind taking hold of everything that's out of control and telling you its ok. Just kiss the problems. It's okay, just hug your circumstances. It's okay, be still with your fragile mind and comprehend that no one has to understand except you. Why live and let the world crush you, when you can die and free yourself of the country that hates you?

The highest form of meditation is to lose the world and all its material possessions and lust. Only through death can you achieve such a freedom and win. I got it *Nirvana*. At least that's what my mind told me, as I stood behind this tree. I soul searched a numb vessel, as I wondered if my soul was Black also. I would hate to be indicted twice.

But I could never commit suicide. It's not fair to those left behind that loved you, supported you, wanted more for you, and made plans that included you.

W.E.B. DuBois contemplated suicide for the entire Black race. He questioned whether or not it would be better than living in a country that, as he thought, could never love us and won't ever love us; hence his move to Ghana. American't has a slavery problem; taking us through slavery, to loitering laws, to Jim Crow, to mass incarceration and the corporate plantation. I wish American't would identify its problems to bring resolution to its addiction to slavery, because the addiction thrives.

Was Greek trying to escape his marriage or slavery? Greek only feigned ignorance, but we've had conversations that proved otherwise. But ignorant or not, even Greek knew we were slaves. The thought made me smile. Greek's oldest daughter was singing, but I still couldn't hear anything, so I allowed my mind to continue deliberating.

I wished W.E.B. DuBois received a federal holiday. We should all celebrate a man who gave us the blueprint for a civil rights movement. But he was bigger than just a movement for Blacks; he was the epitome of 'Knowledge.' I laughed and opened my eyes. Greek hated when I began my rants on Black history. I thought of Black, historic giants, ignored by white history and diminished by the white realities of their time. So, they died twice. DuBois understood. He always understood Black plight.

> *Blacks were born American in American't,*
> *but it wasn't with rights.*
> *Blacks were only allowed to exist,*
> *but we weren't meant to exist with equality.*
> *Blacks were given his-story,*
> *and yet, our contribution got less than a paragraph.*
> *Blacks were told to pursue happiness,*
> *but it wasn't our version of happy, we had to make the white*
> *folk smile.*
> *Blacks were told to work hard,*
> *but it wasn't our work, we didn't own the plantations.*
> *Blacks were told to dream,*
> *but it wasn't our dreams, we had to include the white folk, even*
> *during sleep.*
> *Blacks were told to be free,*
> *but it wasn't our freedom.*
> *In freedom we would never choose slavery,*
> *and today we are still SLAVES!*

If you are Black, you are still a slave. I didn't want to die on a plantation, and I disagreed with Wounded Society. I refused to wait my turn to be shot by a white cop. I didn't want nine minutes and twenty-nine seconds of my life to be determined by a white knee. American't will not kill me. I may have no freedoms in this white sewer, but I will take the freedom to choose my death, or choose not to die in American't.

I can hear Greek's voice telling me to SHUT UP! I laughed and allowed tears to create a stream down my face, across worried, wrinkled skin.

I spoke out loud.

"I love you Greek! I had to give you one last Black history rant before you left me for good. I really wished you would've spoken to me brother, or spoken to one of us."

I pulled out my handkerchief to wipe my face and dry my eyes. I turned and put my back against the tree. People walked to their vehicles and my FAMU brothers were huddled up with their wives and children. I hoped Petra would leave early enough to allow me time to join my brothers and have a moment. But I'm convinced that she knows that I'm somewhere out here, and she is determined to remain seated until I leave first.

I slid down the tree and onto my butt. I stopped trying to control my emotions and let everything out. I stopped wiping the tears away and let them fall. Whatever came out of my nose, so be it. I was tired of hiding from myself.

My name is Nganga Nyjuan Nzumbi.

I should've known Greek was hurting, or did my own pain blind me? My mind flooded with all the things I should've done that could've possibly prevented Greek from taking his life. What kind of friend am I? I closed my eyes and shook my head.

My name is Nganga Nyjuan Nzumbi.

I moved from behind the tree, and took a final look at Greek's casket. Everyone was gone except Petra and her children. She sat emotionless, staring in my direction.

"I apologize Petra." I whispered into the air as I turned to leave.

I should have known better.

If anyone could have seen me this far away, it would a Black woman.

26

I RETURNED THE car to the now closed rental car company, and called a Lyft to take me home. After a long, hot shower, I stretched out on the couch and thought about what I wanted to do.

By morning, I had an idea. I decided to call Nice Head for his opinion.

"Good morning, this is Attorney Nicely. How may I help you?"

"Bro, it's me," I said, confused by his greeting.

"Awe man, I got my cell phone forwarded to my home office, and I didn't look at the caller id. What's up man, we missed you yesterday. Greek's funeral was hard, man. I mean real hard. I was good up until we stood at his grave site. Then we all broke down, one-by-one."

"I was there, you just didn't see me. It was Petra's request and for once, I listened to a Black woman. I hid behind a tree and sneak peeked every now and then. I saw everyone, and I was going to send a group text, but changed my mind. I broke down too man. It's still hard to believe that none of us saw anything like this coming. You know?"

I asked in a way that allowed me to divide the guilt up on my shoulders and share pieces with the other brothers.

Hamilton got the message, "Yeah, we all have a responsibility for watching out for each other. But you should have come over, Bro. Once the funeral started, Petra wouldn't have said anything."

"If I would've walked my black ass over there, there would have been TWO FUNERALS! That woman hates my guts. There was no way in HELL I was showing my face. Damn all that. I'm just going to act like you didn't even say that to me."

Nice Head chuckled.

"Check this out Bro," I continued. "I know this might come as a surprise, but your boy got kicked off the plantation."

Hamilton screamed, "YO! I WALKED OFF THE PLANTATION! All the education in the world and all they see is our skin tone. We can articulate, but they don't hear it. We can dress like them, but they don't see it. Even with a prominent title such as 'attorney' I'm still Black. All of my reports get kicked back two and three times, and not because they are structurally or grammatically incorrect. And not because I don't do a good job making my case. The bottom line is that our skin color stains everything we do, and arouses unnecessary scrutiny."

"When I speak, I'm doubted and challenged, and when I produce, it's viewed as substandard in relation to the white boys I work with. I'm smarter than all of those pink crackers at my firm, and I know it. FUCK all those Ivy League schools. Most of them rode their family names into that office. I earned my way in there. I'm done being an assimilated Negro. That shit is for the birds. We will never be respected in this country. It really makes me wonder if college was worth it?"

"This is BEAUTIFUL!" He yelled. "The world is ours; what you wanna do Black man? All those talks about Black this and Black that, come on Black man, lead the way and I'll follow."

"That's what I want to talk to you about. I'm going to take a sixty day sabbatical and go to Ghana. Number one, I need to clear my head, and number two, I need to come up with a plan. And you know that I want you to be a part of the plan, right?"

Hamilton was in agreement with everything I said. "I can wait sixty days. I want a month to relax and play around with some ideas myself. You need me to do anything while you're away?"

"You already know I do. Check on the condo for me. Take care of a brother's mail and answer the phone when I call." I laughed.

"Always and every time. When you plan on leaving?"

"This weekend. The sooner I can get on a plane, the better. I just need a change of scenery for a while."

"Can you do me a favor while you're over there, please?"

Nice Head breathe a heavy sigh into the phone.

I said, "Of course."

"Can you PLEASE, PLEASE, PLEASE stay away from the women? Single or married, PLEASE!"

I heard him smile through the phone.

Greek's ghost appeared in front of me screaming, "YOU'RE A FUCKING HYPOCRITE!"

My heart skipped a beat and I closed my eyes.

"Yo Nice, I want to come clean about something that only Greek knew. That man committing suicide made me wonder how many secrets he had? And were those secrets the cause of his plight? What I'm saying is this, I'm not thinking about jumping off any bridges, but there is something that I want you to know and I'll even open up more about it when all of the brothers get together again."

My mouth got dry and I had to stand up.

"I uh...." I cleared my throat. "I paid for a lot of abortions from a multitude of women. Y'all have families and I don't. I just don't know if that somehow degrades my character by not telling y'all sooner. Or if I'm somehow weaker than the ideal of me that you hold, personally. I guess what I'm trying to get off my chest is, I'm not perfect. My shit stinks. And instead of trying with one woman, I ran from all of them."

I waited to be judged, and then continued.

"I said I'm going to clear my mind, not make it worse. The last thing I want is to bring a woman into my life. You have my word on that."

I held crossed fingers up to the phone as if he watched, and laughed to myself.

"But who's going to tell the African cuties to stay away from me?"

We both laughed.

"And I just want to say that everyone really looked good standing with your families yesterday. It almost made me want to, kind of, sort of, I don' know.... imagine getting married."

I rolled my eyes.

Nice Head blew a long breath into the phone, and inhaled.

"We all got secrets, man." Another loud exhale.

"But if you feel like you need to get something off your chest to feel better, please do before thinking about hurting yourself. But now that you told me this, I do have one question for you to answer."

Silence again.

I heard my own heartbeat.

I stopped breathing and pushed the cellphone harder onto my ear.

"Obviously thinking about the abortions makes you feel inadequate. You never made the opposite decision to keep and raise a child; regardless of your situation with the mother. If you're really in your feelings about this, I have a question. Hypothetically speaking; if a woman called you as soon as we hung up, and told you she was pregnant, what would you do? Would an abortion be the first alternative to enter your mind?"

And then my brother let me off the hook.

"Maybe you shouldn't give me an answer right now," he said. "But the answer to that question RIGHT NOW, is the only thing that matters. This is definitely one of those topics to get the other brothers involved. You might be surprised; maybe one or two of them possess the same secret."

That statement caught me off guard. I was about to ask if he was one of those brothers, but then bit my lips and remained silent.

Nice Head continued, "And as far as marriage is concerned, whenever the time comes, and you make that decision, I will be standing by your side as the best man, with our brother, Silent Saint, at the pulpit. But one more question for you; Why Ghana?"

Chapter Twenty-Six

I delivered an exasperated response.

"Do you listen to anything that I say? It's where W.E.B. DuBois emigrated once he made the decision to leave American't. As his biggest fan, it's only right that I go pay homage to his memorial."

"Why do I always think of you as a Booker T. Washington Negro?"

He tried to hold his laughter, but happy with his own joke, he chortled loudly.

I dropped my cell phone to my side and looked around the room. I shook my head and put the phone back to my ear. His laughter continued.

"That's fucked up, Bro. You know damn well I don't fuck with dude. You got me on that one. But the second reason that I'm leaving for Africa, is that I realize that I need to grow up."

Now he sat in the silent seat of our conversational seesaw.

After what felt like a full minute, he replied, "That's big. Acquiring that type of introspection, you might actually be maturing already."

"Well its true my brother, I need to grow up."

I stood in the mirror of my foyer.

I took the cell phone off my ear and brought the mic even closer to my mouth, so that Nice Head would hear me loud and clear.

I held my head high in the mirror and said, "My name is Nganga Nyjuan Nzumbi! In case you forgot!"

27

IT HAD BEEN two months since Silent Saint's encounter with the Polk family. It had been two months since he ignored the bishop's phone call; and all the other calls the days after. He sat on the deck of his house, watched his grandchildren play, and read his bible.

Suddenly, he heard a voice, "A scripture a day, keeps the devils away."

He didn't have to turn around to know that it was the bishop.

"Proverbs 18:19," Saint spoke without looking at his guest. "A brother offended is harder to be won than a strong city: and his contentions are like the bars of a castle."

He kept his gaze away from the man who sat next to him, and continued observing his two grandchildren as they dug into the dirt. He smiled then closed his bible and hugged it. He refused to say anything further until the bishop spoke.

"I come in peace," the bishop held out hands and smiled.

He waited for a reply that didn't come. Several minutes passed and the bishop still waited. He wasn't used to being ignored, and Saint knew the bishop felt uncomfortable at the silent treatment. Another several minutes passed, and the bishop joked.

"Well now I know why they call you Silent Saint." He chuckled by himself.

After more silence, he continued, "We've missed you at services. You've placed me in quite a pickle with your immaturity pertaining to the nonsense concerning the Polk family."

Silent Saint raised his right hand up to quiet the bishop.

"You knew that they would call me a nigger if I knocked on their door; didn't you?"

He finally turned his head to look his former employer in the eyes.

"You did everything that you could think of to protect THEM! You know how they feel about Black people, and yet you kiss their ass and continue to take their money. Almost half the church is Black. How many more?"

The men's eyes locked on one another. The bishop broke his glare and returned his gaze forward.

Silent Saint demanded, "How many more of our white, congregation members despise Black people outside of church grounds? Or maybe on it, as if it mattered?"

He rose to his feet. His anger would not allow him to remain sitting.

"Praying with me. Holding my hands. Calling me brother to my face. Crying on my shoulder? How do I walk back into a church not knowing which white person I can trust? IF ANY!"

"EASY! THAT'S HOW!"

The bishop squirmed in his seat and then wiped his mouth. He glanced out into the yard, hoping neither of the children heard his outburst.

"I'm not God. Unbeknownst to me, you seemed to have placed me on a pedestal. So, forgive me for falling off. There is no such thing as a perfect Christian. You know this. It's not for me or YOU to judge."

Now the bishop stood.

"Who gives us money does not matter. And where the money came from does not matter."

He paused staring into the eyes of his confused friend.

"We take from those who are willing to give."

Saint patted the bible against his chest with his left hand, as he said, "The money is one thing, but my humanity is another. I can't be fake. As a Black Pastor and spiritual leader, I can't act like I'm not wondering what a white man or white woman is thinking in front of me. Am I a Pastor or a NIGGER?"

His chest ballooned and he brought the bible to his lips, in an effort to forgive himself for using such an ugly word. He closed his eyes and shook his head to a silent prayer."

The bishop moved closer to Silent Saint, and said, "You're one of the best Pastors that we have." He corrected himself. "You're the best Pastor that we have. You're completely responsible for creating the multicultural congregation that sits in our pews."

Silent Saint snapped, "And how much money is that worth to you? We can be Christian as long as we keep putting something in the collection plate for massa. I never thought that I would taste racism. Call me foolish or naive. But I actually believed that if I became a Christian and stayed away from an all-Black sanctuary, that I could escape my color. That color would dissipate as soon as I walked through those church doors. She didn't just hurt my feelings. Ms. Polk SHATTERED MY REALITY! I told the worst lie that a man could tell. And that's a lie to himself."

He turned his back on the bishop and hung his head.

The bishop raised his hands then let them fall. He was at a loss for words.

Silent Saint raised his head but didn't turn around. He clutched his bible tightly.

"When no one Black is around and someone white tells a nigger joke; do you laugh? I need to know."

Saint kept his body straight and turned his head toward his grandchildren. He refused to shed tears in the presence of the bishop. Looking at his grandchildren gave him the strength he needed to remain resilient. He shook his head and finally turned around to face the bishop.

He moved as close as he could. The wind could barely squeeze between them. He saw fear in the bishop's eyes. He held his gaze, standing eye-to-eye and chest-to-chest, Saint repeated his question.

"When no one Black is around and someone white tells a nigger joke; do you laugh? I-NEED-TO-KNOW!"

He continued his stare into the bishop's eyes, in search of a soul.

The bishop answered frantically.

"One of the many administrative duties requires me to raise money privately to ensure the solvency of the sanctuary. The collection plate alone could never be enough for all of the bills. So, I sit in private with the more influential families for larger donations. Just because it's a church does not mean there is no mortgage. No electric bill. Water bill. Food to be cooked and all the supplemental supplies needed to prepare the food. Field trips for the children and on and on and on. I pray when I have to pray, and I laugh when I have to laugh. Believe it or not, a church is STILL a business. My personal feelings and beliefs are that you people are just as Christian as I am."

Saint smirked.

"I've never complained once as more of your kind grew in membership. Filling our pews. Or invoking your songs. Every person of color has always been treated well by everyone else; especially the white members."

"Me and my kind will be leaving your church. Me and my kind cannot sit next to people who silently think we are less than they are, but like taking our money. These past few weeks I have been talking to MY PEOPLE about what happened. Of course, not one hundred percent of us will be leaving, but the majority is. The veil has been removed. I will no longer lie to myself, my wife, my children or their children. If we are going to be niggers. We will be niggers together and we will pray together, in our own sanctuary away from YOU PEOPLE!"

The white man turned auburn red.

He shook his head to help gather his thoughts.

Then he took a deep breath and spoke.

"Once you get your own church. There will come a day when you'll have a ten thousand dollar problem. You're going to pray to God to help deliver a miracle to you."

The bishop raised his finger to Silent Saint, "The answer to your prayer is going to be someone that you despise. In that moment, you'll have to make a decision. Do you accept the money from someone that you don't like because of your OWN JUDGMENT, that you've placed on their spirit? Acting in the capacity of GOD ALMIGHTY HIMSELF!"

He gestured a finger in Saint's face and continued.

"Or do you let your prayers go unanswered, and lose everything that you've built because you don't have the money? And the people that you DO LIKE, don't have the money and can't financially help you."

The bishop gave his friend time to weigh his words. He took a step back.

"No my friend, the veil is still there. If only good people showed up for church, would we really even need a church?"

The bishop gave Silent Saint a menacing facial expression.

"Huh! I'll be praying for your success."

He turned to leave.

Silent Saint simply replied.

"And I'll be praying for yours too."

28

I **BOOKED A** Monday flight to give me a weekend to run errands and get things in order prior to leaving. I walked off the elevator and Keisha's husband was pacing in front of their open door. When he saw me walking towards my condo he stopped and stared at me. I gave him a head nod and turned to place my key in the door.

"Have you seen my wife, Johanna?" he asked me.

I gave a contorted face and replied, "I thought your wife's name was Keisha."

He placed his hands on his hips.

"Hell no! I don't date Black women, Bro. And don't you think Keisha is a name that's way too Black for a white woman to possess. My wife's name is Johanna."

He laughed, "What's whiter than Johanna?"

I smiled then hunched my shoulders.

"I have no idea where I got that name from. Maybe she has a friend named Keisha."

I thought to myself, *that bitch got me.*

"Hell, I don't know."

"Sometimes she gets mistaken for being Black because of her complexion, but she's whiter than white. NOBODY'S Black in her family."

Emphasis noted. He sporadically and repeatedly turned towards the interior of his apartment, as if his wife would crawl out of a space he overlooked. Then back at me.

I couldn't help it; the historian in me had to retort.

"Technically, there is no such thing as a white person. That was invented to separate the Caucasian poor from interacting with the Black poor by the Europeans in power at the time. Also, science has proven that rape was so rampant in this country between the slave master and his Black slave women, that it's impossible for any Caucasian born in this country to not have some Negro in their bloodline. So technically, if you really want a pure, white, snow bunny, you're going to have to travel to a Nordic country, Bro. I'm just saying. Everyone that looks Black in this country is Black. But everyone that looks white in this country is actually Black also. Or they have some percentage of Black in them, regardless of how they may look on the outside."

I smiled and took a drink from my water bottle.

"Now if we go back to their specification on what it means to be Black in this country. They would all be measured by the 'ONE DROP RULE;' which means that if you possess at least one drop of Black blood in your body, then YOU ARE A NIGGER! Therefore, everyone in this country is Black, purely based on its on racist history."

I smiled again.

"Now that's your lesson for today. I know this is the longest we've ever spoken to one another, and I'm not hating on interracial relationships. I disagree with Umar Johnson on that note. But we are just two Black men talking. What made you decide to not marry a Black woman, anyway?"

The entire time I spoke, I got that weird feeling again. The way he looked at me; he was drooling. I've had gay men stare at me like this before. And if he's gay, that would definitely explain his wife's frustrations and validate her story. Even though she still lied about her name to me. He turned as if he was going into his condominium, but actually walked in a circle.

Chapter Twenty-Eight

"I don't know. My parents were bourgeois Negros. Upper class. I wasn't allowed to play with the ghetto kids, so I never really dated a Black woman to give you an answer. Nor was I ever allowed to bring a Black girl home, so I stayed away from them. And private schools definitely didn't have many, if any, to choose from. Besides, white women look better, right?"

He beamed a smile at me.

I never smiled back.

And suddenly, I had a rush of joy from all the time I fucked his wife. I heard about Negroes like this, but this was my first time interacting with a Black man that despised Black women.

"You know what's ironic about your story?"

He moved back and raised an eyebrow but remained silent.

"Is it your mother that's Black?"

He gave a head nod in the affirmative.

I turned and placed my key in the door to open it. I was half way in and half way out of my condo when I turned around again.

"So, Black women can't really be that bad can they? And I'm sure you don't think she's ugly, right?"

I shot a fake smile in his direction while shooting him with a pointed finger. Then I closed my condo door in his face. He was subdued, but I'm sure he didn't like what I said.

I got ready to shower and replayed our conversation.

After the hot water hit me, I closed my eyes and laughed.

"Yep!" I said to the showerhead. "THAT MOTHERFUCKER GAY!"

29

BIG BRAINS WAS sitting on the airplane waiting for takeoff. He would head to Malaysia for two months, then Vietnam for two months, and then Germany for four months before he could go home for a four-month break before resuming his travels. He closed his eyes and thought about his wife and kids, whom he promised to Facetime on a daily basis.

His wife was not interested in the Asian countries but would be meeting him in Germany for a month. He then thought about an idea he was formulated. Something nagged in the back of his mind. He hadn't put everything together, but the internal wheels of his genius had spun.

He pulled out his iPhone to type some notes, when the Captain came over the intercom.

"We apologize for the inconvenience but due to maintenance, we're going to have to ask everyone to exit the plane. They're going to taxi in a new one, switch the luggage from the old plane to the new one, and then we'll try this again. We apologize for the inconvenience; however, on your way off the plane, we are offering a snack bag with a bottle of water, a bag of peanuts, and some cookies. Thanks for flying Atled."

Big Brains exited the plane with a smile.

This had to be a sign. He rushed over to the gate representative.

"Good morning. I just wanted to know, if I decided that I no longer wanted to fly, can I get my luggage back now?"

After she punched some keys and made Big Brains fill out a form, he was headed for the airport exit. He called his wife and laughed when she answered the phone.

"I just quit my job."

"Did something happen?" his wife asked, in total shock.

Big Brains was still smiling when he answered.

"Yes it did. I have an idea."

Kavonnie Brix was in his office talking to a prospective client, when his wife's father walked in. It wasn't a shock. He'd made visits before.

KayBee held up a finger and Mr. Ocklin walked over to the window with both hands in his pocket. He was wearing a very nice, grey suit with brown shoes that matched his belt. Observing his father-in-law, KayBee was sure that he didn't pick his outfits himself.

His wife also picked all of his clothes, due to years of watching her mother do the same for her father. It was an assumption, but he was confident that he was right. He hung up the phone and stood.

"Good afternoon Mr. Ocklin. What brings you to my neck of the woods, Sir?"

Mr. Ocklin turned around to walk towards KayBee's desk. He sat in one of the two chairs facing his son-in-law. His jaw tightened. KayBee felt the tension; it was palpable. He sat down again, as he remembered his wife asking him not to stand too close to her father because, KayBee's size made him feel insecure.

"You and my daughter have been married for almost twenty years now. What are your plans to give me more grandchildren?"

KayBee smiled.

"We were just discussing this, actually. And we both think it's time."

Mr. Ocklin stared intensely at Kavonnie.

"Let me be frank," he said. "You have two Black children between you now. I want the rest of the children to be white. And I mean white. Not half-white, half-Black. Just white. My wife and I have gone to a sperm bank and read several profiles. We've taken Maddy and she has made her decision on a white donor."

Kavonnie was sure his heart had stopped beating.

"You've already discussed this with my wife?"

Mr. Ocklin was smug.

"We've already discussed this with our daughter. She was our daughter before she met you. And she'll be our daughter whenever you leave."

Kavonnie froze. There's no way his wife would betray him like this. It was just too much to fathom.

"When I GET HOME, I'll discuss this with my WIFE! But I'm telling you right now, not no but HELL NO!" The big man stood to intimidate the weaker man.

Mr. Ocklin closed his eyes and raised a hand.

"You're a good kid. This is no offense to you. We didn't say anything about the first two, but we believe that we should have a say so on the rest of our grandchildren. We'll still love the first two, of course that won't change."

KayBee came from around his desk, moved a chair back and faced it directly across from his father-in-law. He sat down and tapped his desk with his right hand. He needed time to gather his words.

"What is this really about?"

"Legacy," Mr. Ocklin answered. And I don't want my legacy to fall in the hands of....uh.... you people. Your race doesn't have the best track record with finances. My wife and I have amassed a nest egg in excess of forty-million dollars. And if my daughter wants to stay in the Goddamn will, she will comply with this request, with or without you."

Mr. Ocklin rose from his seat.

"It's nothing against you personally. We're not racist people." He smiled. "After all, we did allow you to marry our daughter, and we voted for Obama TWICE. No couple is more liberal in their politics than me and Louise."

He walked towards the door and placed both hands back in his pants pockets. He stopped and turned around.

"But I must admit. I'm very surprised that you're still together. I didn't think Black guys stayed around after the baby was born." He laughed to himself. "I damn sure lost that bet." Removing his left hand from a pocket, he held up two fingers, "TWICE!"

KayBee remained sitting. He didn't know if he should be mad at his wife, her family or both. The big man got up and walked to the window facing downtown. He thought marrying a white woman would place him on a platform higher than marrying a Black woman ever could. He thought he would get the better job, the whiter friends, and enter a world of white people that fascinated him. How far would he go to be accepted by the Oklin family?

The Black man loved his wife.

But now he wondered if she actually loved him?

30

I ARRANGED FOR Nice Head to pick me up and drop me off at the airport to give us time to go over everything. I tried calling everyone else but got voice mails, so I left parting messages. Making sure all the brothers knew where I was going and how long I'd be gone. Once I got comfortable in my first class booth, I reread my father's note.

Nganga Nyjuan Nzumi.

When my mother was alive, she'd cook very big meals for just the three of us. When my father changed his name, my mother refused to change hers. But, astonishingly to me, she allowed my father to name me. After dinner, just him and I would watch television together or play chess. Back then he would drink. And I always knew when he was drunk because he would talk louder and louder.

My favorite memories growing up were when my dad would get drunk and yell at me, "WHAT'S YOUR NAME!"

He never waited for me to reply. But I'd watch him in awe, standing with no shoes on, in the middle of the couch.

He'd go on historical rants that I wouldn't understand until much later; drunk or sober, I could feel the significance of his words. The significance of Black history. Not just because he repeated himself and told the same stories every time that he got drunk. It was because he also purchased Black history books for me.

At first he paid me to read these books. But as I got older, more appreciative and hungrier for knowledge about my own people, I started buying Black history books myself. There were, of course, more favorable, historic rants than others. But I held tight to one particular rant much more than others.

"WHAT'S YOUR NAME!"

I would reply with a smile, "NGANGA NYJUAN NZUMI!"

On this particular day, my father hopped off the couch, which he treated as his podium, grabbed my shirt and twisted it hard into his hands. He lifted me off the floor and brought my small body up close to his face.

"We are slaves. All Black people in this country are slaves. This is something that you have to recognize, acknowledge and then deal with. There'll be many Black men and Black women that are going to try to get you to protest. Somebody Black getting killed. Maybe a piece of legislation that they believe will help Black plight."

"But I want you to remember this until the day that you die, we are slaves!"

"Black people wear the stamp of ownership through their last names. The first thing that white slave masters did after they purchased US, was give US their LAST NAME! That name is a FUCKING BILL OF SALE!"

"And that stamp is going to follow you as long as you are alive in this country. There is no PINK CRACKER going to give a Black man reparations and your bill of sale is his last name. There is no respect in that. And you will be a fool if you try to make him respect you."

"How the FUCK I'mma view you different and your last name is the same as mine or similar."

He stared hard with bulging eyes.

"DO NOT PROTEST WITH NEGROES THAT STILL WEAR A BILL OF SALE! That is a weakness that will get you and them NOWHERE!"

Chapter Thirty

He held me higher, this time with his arm stretched high above his head.

"WHAT IS YOUR NAME!"

I felt the power of this moment and knew that I shouldn't smile.

"NGANGA NYJUAN NZUMI!"

"You might be a slave. But you're a free slave. No white man will be able to hear an American last name and trace you back to a plantation. When a white man hears your name, do you know what he is going to think to himself?"

I stared down into my father's eyes and gave an honest ten-year-old reply.

"No Sir."

With his free hand he poked me in the chest.

"That white man will look at you, hear your name and think but two things. That nigga FREE! And he must be an AFRICAN KING!"

Once when I was sixteen, my dad and I were playing dominoes.

"There has to be more to being free than just changing our names, or giving us African names. I've read a lot of books. But what do I do now?" I asked.

My father smiled.

"Go home. Go to Africa. Once you get there, that's when the magic starts. All of your questions will be answered. A Black man cannot find his identity here. Because your identity is NOT HERE!"

This is the memory that I'll hold on to of my father. This is the memory I'll carry across the ocean until I step foot on my true native land. And when I walk off the plane, I'll inhale the freshest of air while exhaling my name.

I'll feel the freedom that my father often spoke about. I'll understand the passion that DuBois led with. And as I begin to retrace the steps of my ancestors, I'll establish a resolution with myself.

I WILL NOT DIE IN AMERICAN'T!

I WILL NOT DIE ON ANYONE'S PLANTATION!

MOVING FORWARD—I WILL LIVE AND DIE A FREE BLACK MAN!

King Bell aka Jerome Nyjuan Bell, Sr. is an avid reader. He received his undergrad in Business Administration from Florida Agricultural and Mechanical University in Tallahassee, Florida in 1999. He would go on to exit the United States Marine Corps, after serving ten years, and receive his Master's in Business Administration from Averett University in Danville, Virginia in 2003. Mr. Bell is an Entrepreneur and Real Estate Investor who resides in Fayetteville, North Carolina.